PRAISE FOR
OFFER ME A FLOWER

"A magical, mystical thriller that initiates the reader into the beauty of the dark and the light. Grounded in real-life drama, each page carries wisdom and guidance for the seeker. I couldn't put it down."

— WINTER ROBINSON
Author of *Intuitions: Seeing with the Heart* and
Remembering: A Gentle Reminder of Who You Are

"A heartfelt, magical story that you can get lost in and never want to come out! I offer Savitri Bess a flower for weaving a tale that not only takes us on quite a journey but also has such profound truths in it."

— PATRICE KARST
Author of *God Made Easy*

ALSO BY SAVITRI L. BESS

The Path of the Mother: Out of the Shadow into Love
(BALLANTINE BOOKS, 2000)

Offer Me a Flower

A SPIRITUAL QUEST

SAVITRI L. BESS

ILLUSTRATED BY CARAGH MCAULEY

BHARATI IMPRESSIONS
SANTA FE, NEW MEXICO

Published by: Bharati Impressions
               7658-C Old Santa Fe Trail
               Santa Fe, NM 87505

Editors: Sean Murphy and Ellen Kleiner
Book design: Janice St. Marie
Book production: Erin Kathleen Geddie
Cover design and production: Christinea Johnson
Illustrations: Caragh McAuley

A Blessingway book

Publisher's Cataloging-in-Publication Data
Bess, Savitri L.
        Offer me a flower / by Savitri L. Bess;
     illustrated by Caragh McAuley. — 1st ed.
        p. cm.
        LCCN: 98-94861
        ISBN: 0-9668373-8-X

        1. Spiritual life — Fiction. 2 Self-realization —
     Fiction. 3. Femininity of God — Fiction.
     I. McAuley, Caragh. II. Title.

PS3552.E79485O44 1999   813'.54
                    QB199-16

10 9 8 7 6 5 4 3 2 1

This book is dedicated
to Mother's children everywhere

WITH GRATITUDE

To my beloved guru,
Mata Amritanandamayi;

To the musicians
who wrote the music and lyrics for the Santa Fe Satsang tapes
and CDs—Luce's inspiration in moments of need;

To my editor
Sean Murphy, Adjunct Professor, University of New Mexico
at Taos, without whose encouragement and expertise this book
would not have come to fruition;

To everyone who graciously read
the manuscript and offered precious suggestions:
Tito Naranjo, Harvey Blaustein, Prema Heindmarch,
Gunavati Lowe, Sandhya Kolar, Karuna Poole, Ahmayo Bohm,
Maureen Walsh, and my sister, Elizabeth Smyth;

To Ellen Kleiner,
whose remarkable skill in editing,
production, and publishing were invaluable. Ellen's loving care
as the midwife, the blessingway guide, gave me confidence
throughout all stages of the publication process.

CONTENTS

CHAPTER ONE
Angels in the Snow 9

CHAPTER TWO
The Search 17

CHAPTER THREE
A World Collapsing 33

CHAPTER FOUR
Inextricably Entwined 51

CHAPTER FIVE
A Sideshow of Magic Spells 71

CHAPTER SIX
Sidetracked by the Macabre 95

CHAPTER SEVEN
River of Fire 119

CHAPTER EIGHT
The All-Devouring Universe 137

CHAPTER NINE
Offer Me a Flower 159

Chapter One

Angels in the Snow

I watched her disappear behind the giant saguaro cactuses, her white garments flapping in the breeze, fading into the desert like a shimmering mirage. A cactus wren whistled in the distance. The sun rising over the mountains warmed my back and lit up the sea of yellow palo verde blossoms in the valley below. I squinted, searching for her, but she was gone. Closing my eyes to savor her afterglow, I pondered her words, wondered where to begin and how much she wanted me to reveal.

Perhaps it's best to start with the swans. I was five the year I saw them, white and glistening on the water. My father had left home that year, and soon afterward my grandfather died. My mother took me to the funeral in Minnesota on a Pullman train. The old man lay with pasty face and bushy mustache in a strange wooden box. When Mom lifted me to see him I stared, unable to figure out why he was so plastic- looking, why he didn't really seem to be there. Although I felt the sticky stillness in the air, death itself was meaningless to me.

One gray afternoon a few days later, we drove with my aunt Gretchen to a lakeside park where I was free to roam as I pleased. Swells lapped onto the shore, in contrast to the rush of ocean waves I was used to in California. Then out of the mist, three swans floated toward the beach like majestic beings out of some fairy tale. As they drifted closer, I imagined myself riding one into the sky, my arms clasped around its neck, the wind blowing into my face. When they reached land, they waddled over to me. A thrill ran through me when one poked its soft beak into my palms, tickling, nuzzling, then tugging at my coat. In my mind it wanted to take me to its magic kingdom where swans and angels play. But all at once my mother shrieked and raced toward us, waving her arms, apparently afraid the swan was going to pull me into the lake. A lump came to my throat as the great white birds flapped their wings, honked, and glided away. *I won't get to meet a swan princess after all.*

In California we often spent weekends and holidays at our mountain cabin in Pine Hills, where my mother let me scamper outside to wander the mile-long pathways to neighboring houses. Lithe and quick, brown hair always slightly disheveled, I would search the paths for animal tracks. Occasionally, I would hear cries like wolves howling through the pines, and I would imitate them, hoping eventually to call one to me so we could be friends and run together in the woods.

One winter day after a newly fallen snow, I paraded down a trail amid firs and oaks laden with white. The only sounds in the soft silence were my boots crunching through the drifts. Bubbles of joy swirled inside my chest. Spontaneously, I burst forth in chantlike repetition: "Walking in a winter wonderland . . . Walking in a winter wonderland."

Suddenly, I froze dead still, hypnotized by a pair of slanted yellow eyes that peered out from an ice-laced manzanita bush, held down by some invisible force. My breath stopped and my heart pounded against my chest. Then tufts of fur sprouted out of the red branches; a pair of ears rose above the slanted eyes; a black nose punctuated a grayish ruff. It was a wolf!

A tingling at the back of my neck sent chills through my body. *I want to touch it.* Like aspen leaves quaking in the wind, my hands trembled as I struggled to pull off my mittens. The wolf stood still like a forest sentinel. After freeing one hand, I held it out, palm up, the empty mitten dangling from its string. The creature inched toward me. "Come on, Mr. Wolf. Don't be afraid," I whispered. "Come here."

It tiptoed closer. In response I crept forward, setting my foot gently into the snow. The wolf raised its pointed nose to sniff, whereupon a puff of cold air rushed from its nostrils. I stepped forward again, but immediately the animal sneered, showing fangs, like a dog protecting its food dish. I jerked my hand away with such force that I fell onto my back in the snow.

I lay there for what seemed like a long time, eyes pinched closed. I could hear the beast trotting around me, and everything inside me trembled. *If we could only play . . . Maybe angel wings. Yes! If I lie here still as a mouse and then move my arms ever so slowly, the wolf will want to play, just like our dog Dandy.* I moved my arms and legs across the snow in the familiar windmill pattern, up and down, back and forth, softly singing, "Angels in a winter wonderland . . . Angels in a winter wonderland." Up and down, back and forth, I continued to trace angels in snow.

The animal growled like a puppy, leapt, grabbed my loose mitten in its teeth. I giggled and moved my arms faster. The creature pounced on my furry hood and tugged at it, dragging me slowly through snowdrifts, shaking its head like a dog pulling a rag toy. Then my parka tightened around my throat, and I became scared. Reaching back to let it be known that my neck was hurting, my bare hand brushed against fur. *I'm touching the wolf!* Right away, my body went limp like a Raggedy Ann doll, and I could feel a warm current racing through my fingers.

I could hear the wolf jumping around, making swooshing noises in the snow, stopping and starting before attacking my knitted mitten again. Then as he held it in his teeth, I pulled my arm just a bit and all at once a pine branch released a pile of snow onto my chest. At first I thought the creature had jumped on me, but the feeling wasn't big like a wolf. Then again, it didn't feel like snow, either. It was soft like a cloud and gentle like a breeze and fragrant like the night-blooming roses in my backyard at home.

When I opened my eyes, I saw a woman in white robes standing at my feet, arms held high like wings bigger than any I had ever made in the snow. *A swan lady!* She was more beautiful than a fairy-tale princess, with eyes that shone black as diamonds and a smile that danced like sunlight on ocean waves. Her brown-skinned hands stretched toward me in the way seedlings reach toward the light. I opened my arms to her and she swooped me up against her soft breast. Tightly, I wrapped my legs around her ample waist and my arms around her neck, my fingers tangling in her long, wavy black hair. I cried, shaking in her reassuring embrace. "I'm not afraid anymore," I whispered at last.

The white-robed woman murmured into my ear, "My precious child."

I buried my head into her shoulder for a while, then unwound my arms, pulled back, and looked at her round face. "Are you an angel?"

The woman giggled, like a brook gurgling over moss. "I am your Mother."

"You don't look like my mother."

"I am everyone's Mother." Her voice rasped, as if squeezing through a muted trombone.

I lifted my eyebrows, smiled, and shook my head. "Not my mom's."

The Mother's teeth glimmered.

I wiggled and slid down her belly, dropping onto the ground. By then the wolf was lying quietly by a granite rock nearby. I looked up at the Mother and slipped my hand into her slender, petal-like fingers. "I want to play with him again. Will you come with me so I can pet him?"

The Mother's body rippled with glee. "Yo! Wild animals can be dangerous." Her fingers, imitating a pony, jumped up and down on my arm. "A colt romps around, kicks its hooves to play, and doesn't understand its game can injure us by accident. So it is with any wild animal." I bounced up and down on my heels and smiled up at the Mother. She stroked my hair and added, "In the wilderness it is wise to be both gentle and cautious."

I glanced at the rock, but the animal was no longer there. "He's gone!" Tugging at the Mother's robes in an effort to pull her toward the boulder, I asked, "Did you see him go? I want to be his friend. Oh, please." I ran around the Mother and then tapped her thigh.

"Will he ever come back?"

"He might. Someday."

I raced over to the rock, peered into the woods, and skipped back to the Mother. "Will you cook me some spaghetti for dinner?"

She laughed, took me by the hand, floated across the snow to an open space surrounded by pines, and laid flat on her back. Up and down, back and forth she brushed her arms and legs across the snow. I quickly joined in the fun, whereupon she leapt up and bounced to another spot. We ran and flopped down in the snow, making all kinds of angels—some with crowns of pinecones, others with snowballs ready to throw, and still others with acorns for eyes. I then tagged along behind my new friend as she wound her way to the center of the winged creations. There she sat cross-legged; I did the same.

The Mother reached over to arrange my hands in prayer position.

"Why are you doing that?" I asked, looking up at her.

She chuckled and her eyes flickered. "Daughter, when you hold your hands like this, I will always come."

"Like this?" I asked, lightly pressing my palms together.

She nodded, then closed her eyes. I closed mine too. In the stillness I felt like a piece of fluff on top of cotton candy. Then the whispering of the breeze through the pines broke the silence. When I opened my eyes, the place where the Mother had been sitting was empty. I jumped up, searched behind several trees, then darted back to the round indentations amid the circle of angels, staring at my spot and at hers, all the while noticing the distinct smell of roses in the air. My eyes probed the forest of snow-laced pines, and I called out, "Where are you?" The wind whined like a distant siren.

My bare hand was numb with cold. Unable to pull the torn mitten on, I placed my hands together the way the Mother had said, and looked up. A dark cloud with black trailings like hair merged into the solid gray sky. "Come back down," I called, desperate for my new friend to hear me. Snowflakes blew every which way, blinding me. I squinted, straining to catch a glimpse of the Mother behind the cloud. "If I find the wolf, will you come again?"

I hung my head, pulled the hood of my parka over my eyes, and ambled down the trail to the cabin. The words "I will always come" echoed through the chilling wind as I picked up speed and scampered down the path. Within minutes of seeing smoke billowing from the chimney of our log cabin, I was throwing open the door. The smell of spaghetti and meatballs filled the air. My mom stood by the rock fire-place, frowning behind her glasses.

"Mommy," I exclaimed, "I saw a wolf, and then a lady in white came to play. We made angels in the snow!"

My mom put her hands on her hips. "Luce, where have you been? Your mitten's torn and you're soaking wet—you'll catch your death of cold. And how'd you rip your hood?"

I ran past the Norman Rockwell prints decorating the walls, past the faded, ranch-style couches and chairs, and right into the tiny kitchen. "Did she make spaghetti?"

"Who? Honey, you're chilled. Go change your clothes and sit by the fire."

Chapter Two

The Search

"How much is that poster of the wolf?" I asked the ranger behind the sales counter at Chiricahua National Monument Visitors Center.

I was embarking on a week alone in the wilderness to search for the Mother. Although I had lost nearly all hope of meeting her again, I refused to relegate my childhood experience of her to mere fantasy. "Luce, you're imagining things again," my mom had said. "There are no wolves in these mountains, honey." But hadn't I gazed into the animal's eyes and touched its fur? The Mother's breast had been so soft, her voice so clear, her laughter so distinct. Nothing in all the intervening years had equaled the joy I felt when the Mother dropped down with that pile of snow. As crazy as it seemed, at age twenty-seven I was intent on resurrecting my childhood belief that if I were to have a close encounter with a wolf, the Mother might reappear.

"It's not a wolf—it's a coyote," said the ranger.

"A coyote?" I stared at the reddish-gray fur that sprouted into dark gray, the cream-colored ruff, the yellow eyes. The coyote looked exactly like the wolf I had played with when I was five years old. Certainly, the beast in this picture seemed larger and grayer than the countless coyotes I had seen in the Arizona desert. My mind danced with images of the wolf and of making angels in the snow.

"It's five dollars." The ranger said. "Did you want it?"

"Huh?"

"Do you want the poster?"

"Oh yes, I do. How much is it?"

The ranger rolled her eyes. "Five dollars."

I fumbled through my fanny pack and pulled a five-dollar bill from my wallet.

With the rolled-up poster tucked under my arm, I walked briskly to my Honda Civic and headed for Turkey Creek campground. I was on spring break from the University of Arizona where I was studying for a master's degree in counseling. Over the previous few months I'd been searching for the reason my mind felt like a wasteland of useless thoughts, my heart dry and withered. Not that I wasn't successful, or even joyous at times. But after college I'd floundered around a bit, starting and stopping two graduate programs; then I joined the Peace Corps in Peru.

Now, although I was doing well in the counseling department, sometimes I'd wake up crying, groping after a fading dream. Other times I'd burst into tears for no apparent reason. As much as I probed my mind for the cause of this despair, it seemed to have no logical point of origin. I wondered if it had been triggered by memories of my mother's divorce, or of my own broken relationships. Perhaps so, I concluded, secretly yearning for a more enduring love and for another precious meeting with the Mother.

After that winter in Pine Hills when I was five years old, I'd often fashioned snow figures after her, weaving long hair out of masses of dead pine needles. I'd clasp my arms about her prickly neck and press my cheek against her icy chest, imagining my breath warming her to life. Then I'd hold her invisible hand, and we'd play and dance. One spring day I thought I caught a glimpse of her disappearing behind a manzanita bush. I scrambled through the underbrush, pursuing her, white robes flashing like a deer's tail through the pines. But I found nothing—only the wind rustling the oaks' tender leaves. On other occasions I felt her, hovering and warm, floating behind me down the narrow trail to the cabin. I would creep on soft feet, fearing that if I turned to look she would fade into the breeze. Then unable to withstand the suspense, I would peek over my shoulder, eyes half closed. If she had been there, she'd invariably vanished, leaving only the smell of roses.

Once when I was nine and strolling alone through the fog on sand hardened by the receding tide, I was sure she was there, perched on a distant rock, looking out to the sea. I raced toward her. But when I got there, all I found was a handful of seagulls bunched together, their white breasts blending into the mist. I scurried around the rock, scattering birds, searching for footprints. At last I found one, sinking into the sand under the receding waves.

Now I continued driving along the winding dirt road as it followed a gentle ravine up to the base of the Chiricahua peaks. Turkey Creek campground, at an altitude of 6,000 feet, was nestled in the gully at the end of the road, where the creek bed narrowed and climbed more steeply. With nighttime temperatures still in the low thirties, the site would surely be free of other overnighters. No one crashing through the bushes, talking loudly on the trails, or playing boom boxes. The perfect setting for encountering a wolf— or a coyote, as the case might be.

I pulled into a turnout, unloaded my pack, gave my car a little pat, and hoisted my camping equipment onto my back. To find the trailhead, I slid down the steep rise from the road into the campground, located a log that crossed the creek, and took a path that rose into the wilderness. Breathing in the scent of ponderosa, Chiricahua pine, and piñon, I hiked for about a mile and a half to a hidden spot just off the trail. Rocks were in place from someone else's campfire circle—evidence that I wasn't the first person drawn to this little sanctuary. At night, it would serve as my base camp; during the day, I would explore the woods.

A streamlet lent moisture to the dryness of the high desert. Mossy green patches lined the bed where little fish darted about, catching invisible delectables. My gaze wandered through the veil of translucent green, meandered up crevices separating pine bark wedges, glided across limbs. Yet still my mind pestered me. *How can I feel discontent amid all this beauty?*

My stomach rumbled as I unpacked, pitched my tent, and collected dry wood. I heated water over my propane camp stove to make instant split-pea soup and a pile of noodles. I plopped down under one of the ponderosas and rested my back against the trunk. While I ate, my mind drifted back to making angels in the snow with the Mother. I had difficulty remembering some of her features, but not her eyes, alive as they were with starlight, or her smile, bright like the midsummer sun. The love I felt in her presence rounded me out, leaving none of the rough edges that seemed to come with temporal love.

It was strange that my mom had given no credence to this experience, since she'd always delighted in my creations of poinsettia-leaf sleds for Santa's elves and other acts of fantasy. But my stories of the wolf and the woman in white drew only frowns and a stinging silence. Even my godmother, who used to lead me into the "fairy woods" down the hill from her cabin, said there were no wolves in this part of the country, and certainly no woman in white. When my dad visited, I saw a twinkle in his eye as I told the story, but he said nothing. Life was often barren after that. School teachers wore blank faces. I wrote letters of the alphabet upside down and had difficulty adding numbers. When asked about school on a particular day, I would say that I'd romped through eucalyptus leaves behind the amphitheater, or kicked the ball farther than anyone could catch it.

Sitting under the ponderosa, I finished my noodles. The last twinkle of the sun's light through the pine needles brought a chill to the air. Only a hint of pink and pastel orange remained as twilight's afterglow. I moved swiftly to prepare for night. After storing my food in a net and hanging it from a tree, I put on more layers of clothes, slipped into my down parka, then relaxed by the fire. No moon. No wind. Not even a breeze. No sounds, except for the occasional crackling of firewood and the gurgling of the creek.

"When you hold your hands like this, I will always come." What had the Mother really meant? Picking up a thin stick, I poked it in the fire, pulled it out, and watched it burn. Then I stood up, waving the burning twig in a circular motion around the fire. "I will always come," I chanted. I held the stick up toward the Milky Way and waved it in a circle, drawing a halo around the entire sea of stars, imagining the mass of dotted white to be the Mother. *Oh, Mother, please let me find you again.*

I stepped slowly around the fire circle and sang, "Mother Mary comes to me. There will be an answer. Let it be . . ." Around and around I turned, my fire-stick swirling, sending ghosts of light streaking through the sky like comets. Tossing the burning stick into the circle of rocks, I raised my arms overhead. Beneath the blackest sky dotted with 10 billion stars, I danced until I fell to the ground, arms spread out, palms open to receive their light. The ground seemed to move under me as I gazed at the vast expanse of sky. A mild breeze caressed my face, sending chills throughout my body. When the freezing temperatures became too cold to bear, I dragged myself into my sleeping bag.

Like a ship's bell ringing an alarm, a sound startled me awake—*whippoorwill, whippoorwill!* Again I heard the urgent cry. I unzipped the door of my tent to peer out. The waning moon cast an eerie light over the campsite, sending shivers down the back of my neck. *If I were smart, I would pack up first thing in the morning. But I'm not really here to leave at the earliest sign of discomfort, am I?*

I had learned that birds can be messengers. On the banks of New Mexico's Chama River a lone warbler had once come to my tent before dawn, well before its usual waking hour. Like the rippling arpeggio of a flute, the bird's tune permeated the predawn silence. I knew it had called me out of the cozy nest of my sleeping bag to walk the mile and a half to Christ in the Desert Monastery. Red sand cliffs on the opposite side of the river dwarfed the small Benedictine chapel. The full moon's light floated on the water, casting its glow onto nature's cathedral of sheer rock. I arrived at the sanctuary just before the monks began their early morning chanting. Resting on the steps facing the river, I listened to the droning of men's voices echo through the chapel.

But the whippoorwill's cry was different. It seemed to portend danger. I lay back down, pulled the mummy bag's hood over the top of my head, and gazed at the silhouettes of trees dancing on the tent.

I awoke at first light, and rather than make a fire to warm up, I went straight to boiling water for tea on the camp stove, intent on escaping any impending danger as quickly as possible. With one hand holding the hot cup and the other untying the food net, I spilled the tea and had to boil more water. Newly sliced apples for steaming slipped out of my grip like sardines, tumbling to the dirt before I could catch them. *I wish I knew exactly what that whippoorwill was trying to warn me about. One thing's for sure—I'm not going to wait around to find out.* With the last spoonful of cinnamon-spiced apples still in my mouth, I threw my water filter in the day pack, just in case I'd be stuck in the woods. After checking the pack to make sure it contained everything I'd need for a three-hour hike, I flung it on my back and headed east up the trail into the mountains.

My breath caught in my throat as I hiked at a fast clip. Even so, I didn't slow down until the sun had lit up the tops of the hills behind me. The rising desert sun warmed the air so quickly that I was soon peeling off my parka, turtleneck, and long underwear, and rolling them into the day pack. I enjoyed the freedom of movement I felt in only my lightweight T-shirt and jeans.

Like a deer turning its head this way and that for signs of a predator, I sniffed, watched, and listened. After some time, I sat on a rock, feeling foolish. The Chiricahua Mountains were full of sites for settling down and contemplating the Mother. Too many, perhaps. Without a compass or contour map, I could easily get lost after roaming off the trail for any distance. At that moment, a crow cawed. I leapt off the rock and made tracks up the hill in its direction, thinking maybe its call was a sign. Minutes later, when I saw the black bird soaring swiftly into the canyon, I shook my head. *I should have brought a map. I'll just stick to my original plan of staying close to the trail.*

The murmuring of a stream lured me into the scrub oak underbrush and beyond, where a gentle waterfall emptied into a sandy pool. Dry mosses hung from the branches of piñon pines like vines in a jungle forest. A few ponderosas and Apache pines towered above the small meadow where the stream cascaded over polished rocks. It looked like the perfect place to sit and wait for the Mother.

Although holding my hands in prayer position seemed natural in my younger years when the Mother showed me how, it felt contrived at this stage of my life. In my Italian Renaissance art class I had seen scores of images of human beings in prayer—Mary praying to the angel who announced Jesus' conception, angels supplicating before the baby in the manger, art patrons petitioning the holy beings whose portraits they had consigned. Always, they were crying, imploring, adoring, expressing beatific attitudes. But pressing my hands together and calling aloud to God had not been part of my upbringing. Hence as an adult I felt self-conscious just thinking about following the Mother's instructions.

I bent over the little pond, dipped my fingers into the clear water. It was just deep enough for a refreshing plunge and relief from the midday heat. Large insects with long, spindly legs skated across the surface, casting darting shadows on the sand below. Little fish with tails like flashing whips scurried beneath the shiny rocks.

Snap! A twig broke in the bushes behind me. *Is it my imagination?* I bolted upright and immediately felt a familiar tingling run up and down the back of my neck. In recent years I'd had two encounters with pick-pockets—one while on a bus in Boston and another while traveling by train in Italy—and each time, moments before, I'd felt someone watching me. Although I held onto my purse tightly, in both instances there was a spit second when I let go and the thief seized my wallet.

Again I heard a rustling in the bushes. *Whatever it is, it's big. No lizard or bird would make that much noise.* I inched downstream to a spot where I could cross over easily if I had to. There I remained poised, mentally plotting my move. Once more, dry leaves crackled. I edged down the bank of the stream, poking at rocks with my boot. Another rustle. I swirled my head around. Just behind the oaks that lined the clearing, a man thrust his bushy head through the leaves and crashed forward. I leapt over the stream, bolted like a deer into the woods.

Although athletic, I was no match for this large man. Instinct drove me to scurry first in one direction, then in another, like a rabbit darting away from a huge dog. I dashed under bushes too difficult for the man to negotiate easily, then instead of going forward into a gully, I backtracked noiselessly into a soft patch of grasses. Never once did I look behind; I only listened. Hearing my pursuer thrash down the hill through the underbrush, I headed into a ponderosa grove, where a fallen tree leaning against a sturdy one with low branches provided an opportunity for me to scale the trunk. Adrenaline gave me the force to scramble up it like a cat. There I perched, leaning into the bark to muffle my rapid breathing.

The man had slowed his pace, even stopping on occasion— probably to listen. Now the sounds of bushes scraping and twigs crackling receded toward the gully, whereupon I rested my cheek against the tree and heaved a sigh into the fresh breeze. Then I sucked in hard, holding my breath. *He's circled back!* He plowed through the chaparral, close enough for me to catch a glimpse of him. He was tall, about thirty-five years old, and dressed in a torn camouflage shirt, matching pants, and army boots. His long brownish hair formed dreadlocks that swung as he growled. A moment later he disappeared into the thickets, whereupon the sound of rustling brush came from below, then farther off again. *He must be checking behind every shrub for signs of his prey.* I took mea-sured sips of air as the rumblings of his hunt faded into the distance.

Like a monkey clinging to its mother, I hugged the tree in a full-body hold while my breathing slowly returned to normal. Finally, I took a deep breath, sighed, and began singing softly, like a small child, "We are climbing Jacob's ladder . . . We are climbing higher, higher . . ." Soon I was feeling calmer and safe enough to relax my grip on the tree. All the while, images of the chase replayed in my mind. *I could have been killed. The whippoorwill and the crow must have been warning me not to continue this senseless search.* I wondered if I should simply return home to Tucson, but my heart told me not to give up. *I think I'd rather die than live without the Mother's love.* I held back tears of ambivalence and swung my feet, mindlessly banging them against the tree trunk. *I'll rest here for just a while longer.*

When I finally climbed down, I didn't quite know where I was and didn't want to take chances. Logically, my next move would have been to either go back uphill to the trail I'd be on or head for the gully and follow it westward. Instead, I decided to take several detours to avoid leading the bushman to my base camp. First, I would forge my way east; then I would climb the mountain in hopes of picking up the trail.

Around midafternoon, with the path still nowhere in sight, I crouched under a Gambel oak, ravenously hungry. I fumbled through my pack for the sesame butter sandwich and package of blue corn chips I had tossed in before leaving the campground. There were two apples as well, which I decided to save for later. After gulping down the sandwich and chips, I resumed my search, using the tallest peak as my navigation point. Higher and higher I climbed, picking my way around bushes and occasional Douglas firs, and pausing occasionally to sip precious drops of water, all the while scanning the terrain for evidence of a trail. *It's got to be here somewhere.*

Beads of sweat poured down my face and neck. My mouth was parched, but since the landscape all about me was bone dry I knew I had to conserve the little water that was left. Pangs of worry shot through my chest. It was late afternoon, and the thought of spending the night without a tent or sleeping bag raised goose bumps down my arms and legs. Nor did I relish the idea of missing dinner. But I knew how foolish it would be to plow through the brush at night without even the moon to light my way. On previous treks excitement would course through my bloodstream whenever I contemplated being forced, unprepared, to survive in the wilderness. Not now, however. Not with a crazed man on the prowl.

The sun was only inches from the horizon when I spotted a small cave among a cluster of nearby boulders. Set above a gentle slope, the indentation in the rock was shallow and rectangular— just large enough for my body. The hour after sunset provided enough light for me to settle in. Swiftly, I collected piles of dry wood, then formed a fire circle with the many rocks scattered among the grasses.

I looked and listened before deciding to make a fire. Convinced that I was temporarily safe, I laid dry twigs and pine needles against a large piece of wood, pulled waterproof matches from my pack, and lit one, setting it against the kindling. *Even if he sees smoke, he won't have time to reach me. It's getting too dark. He'll never find his way.* Gently, I coaxed the tiny flame with my breath, adding longer lengths of wood as it grew. My intention was to amass a pile of hot coals to keep me warm through the night, since it would be much colder here than at base camp. Guessing from the firs and occasional aspens that I was at an elevation of about 8,000 feet, I rummaged around in my pack for the survival blanket I always carried with me but never before had to use. The advertisement on the tiny package claimed the paper-thin, metallic-looking space-age material would prevent hypothermia.

The fire crackled softly and burned low enough so as not to attract attention. A diffuse band of pastel orange and rose lined the ridges and flat horizon of the desert below. My hideaway looked out onto a panoramic view of the basin-and-range features, revealing islands of mountains that dotted the Sonoran Desert. To envision the white sand covered by an ocean millions, perhaps billions, of years ago took only a small stretch of the imagination. I was a tiny speck in infinite time, part of a boundless whole.

The vast expanse of mountains, sky, and desert reminded me of the purpose of my visit. At this point, however, I had only enough strength to lift my arms, place my palms together, and sing a dronelike "Please come" before my body slumped over. The world around me blotted itself out as I surrendered to sleep. My chin fell to my chest, momentarily startling me awake. *I forgot to make my bed.* I hoisted myself up, stumbled down the hill, and groped around collecting pine needles for a sleeping pad. Settled at last inside my cave, I knew that hardly anything, including the bare rock for a mattress, could have prevented me from falling asleep.

A piercing *yip, yip, yip* woke me in the middle of the night—the short, staccato notes of coyotes barking in unison. I imagined the intermittent silences to mean they were eating or dragging a small animal home. One lone coyote's drawn-out howl, high-pitched and unearthly, drew me into wildness, sucking me into a hole in space where mysteries disappeared into a velvety blackness. Now that I knew my childhood encounter might have been with a coyote and not a wolf, the eerie call sent a tingling rush of joy through my veins.

Cold air crept through gaps the parka wasn't big enough to cover. Too tired to pile more wood on the dwindling coals, I rolled over stiffly, curled up under layers of space blanket and jacket, and drifted back to sleep.

A symphony of birds from seemingly every branch of every tree mingled with the hazy world of slumber and the stark reality of my cave bed. With that, my mind meandered into wakefulness. I opened my eyes to the blackness that precedes dawn, when the faintest rays of the sun creep around the edge of the earth, warming the sky to a shady indigo. I was only slightly puzzled that I now lay fully stretched out on my back, toasty as a fledgling under its mother's wing. The birds' chorus infused my chamber of rock with celestial strains, as if from hosts of angels. Stretching my legs, I grazed my left knee against a lump. My hand probed from beneath the survival blanket and soon came upon a furry mass. "Eee!" I withdrew my hand like a gopher scooting down a hole, and yanked my parka back over my head. The creature shifted gently against my body. *Oh my God.*

Slowly, I slid the jacket away from my face, peeked down beside me, and sucked in air. *Coyotes! They let me touch them.* There, nestled against me like pups with a mother dog, were three coyotes. The one curled against my left side was studying me through yellow eyes; the other two were wrapped together at my right side, still snoozing. I lay perfectly still, savoring the moment. Then I noticed that mingled with the smell of wild fur and dew on the ponderosas and firs was the scent of rose. Was I still in the same cave? I wondered. On top of the same mountain? The light cast a gentle glow all about us as one of the coyotes got up, stretched, and trotted toward a white form not more than fifteen feet away.

The Mother! I stared in disbelief, fumbled to get out from under my covers, then crawled to my feet, shuffling toward what I feared was only an apparition. As I approached, I could see the Mother sitting cross-legged under a ponderosa on the knoll overlooking the valley, her robes shimmering in the soft light. My heart swelled with a sudden love, much as it had when I was a child. I tiptoed to within several feet of her, crouched down, and also sat cross-legged, afraid to move closer for fear she would disappear. Tears moistened my cheeks as I looked about me with wonder, not knowing if what I saw was real. Everything—the trees, the birds, the grasses—was crystal clear. One coyote lay in front of the Mother, prostrate at her feet, its nose on the ground. The other two sat patiently a few yards off. The Mother's long black wavy hair, together with the dark hue of her face that changed from chocolate to black to chocolate again, contrasted sharply with the thin white cloth draped around her head.

When the first beams of sunlight flashed across the top of the mountain, the Mother stirred, beckoning me to come closer. My heart skipped beats and I hesitated, stepping gingerly toward her, all the while staring as if my gaze would fix her to that spot forever. Her hoarse, mellow laughter bubbled. She motioned for me to sit. I was bursting with so much love I could hardly breathe. As I settled to the ground before her, the coyotes sprang up, trotted forward, and thrust their noses into her lap, nuzzling their heads into the folds of her garments. She stroked them and kissed them between their eyes. One by one, they loped away into the woods. Then she reached over, pulled my head into her lap, and murmured, "My precious child," just as she had done nearly twenty-two years before. I buried my face into her belly, reveling in a joy that extended beyond the confines of time, beyond the moon, the stars, and the blackness of night.

Silence pervaded, except for the birds that, having finished their tribute to dawn, were now chirping and fluttering about. Eventually, I slid my head out from under the Mother's forearm and sat up beside her, cupping my chin in my hand, staring with hazy eyes at the desert below. Seconds passed, maybe entire minutes, as images of the chase through the woods and the danger of spending days without water or food flashed through my mind.

"Daughter, like a candle blown out by the wind, your life can come to an end at any moment. Your body's well-being is not in your hands, for everything happens in its own time. Fledglings break through their shells to come into the care of their mother. Through no fault of its own, one might tumble out of the nest before it is ready to fly. Another might later fall prey to a hawk or eagle. The others may live to raise their own families of birds. All will eventually die."

I frowned, put my fingers to my mouth, and glanced off into the distance, struggling to understand.

She stroked my head and smiled. "Child, the body is only temporary. You are born, grow up, study in school, get a job, raise a family, grow old, and die. Only the soul is permanent. For you to be truly free, the body mustn't be the primary object of concern. The man you saw yesterday might have hurt or killed you, but that wasn't to be your destiny. Even the clever way you escaped was not under your control, although you may think it was. These types of experiences come in order to teach us that there is something beyond the body, mind, and intellect. You sang 'Jacob's Ladder.' Why?"

I whirled my head around to face her. "How did you know? It just came. It made me feel good."

"It reminded you of the only aspect of yourself that never changes—the all-pervading soul, the source of true happiness. Last night you were content not having the comforts of your camp. You even felt joy in the absence of things that ordinarily bring you pleasure. Your only concern was about me and your immediate needs, not the past or the future. The animals sensed your love for them, so they came to keep you warm. They felt your connection to the source of all that is."

The sun had burned away the morning chill. I removed my parka, pulled out the two apples, and offered one to the Mother. She chuckled, took a bite, and gave it back to me.

"You'll go away again, won't you?" I asked. "I like what you tell me, but how can your words help me feel this love when you're *not* around?"

"You will have to surmount a series of hurdles. Each one will remove another veil bringing you closer to me, to the mystery of the immortal nectar."

I paused while chewing. "Immortal nectar? Is that something you drink while dying?"

A burst of rippling laughter propelled the Mother's body off the ground. She looked at me with the smile of a thousand moons, and stroked me under the chin with her delicate fingers. "Daughter, dying is the same as being born; it is only a change. Your yearning to be near me will draw you further and further into yourself. Eventually, you will develop a burning desire to know the immortal nectar. Remain always in the present, as you did yesterday. I will guide you. Surely, you will succeed in reaching the goal."

I pulled my knees up to my chest and clasped my arms around them. "I don't think I understand what the goal is," I replied.

"While it is important to care for our bodies and develop our minds, we must be conscious of the fact that they are impermanent. For now, try to remember that attachment to them is the cause of great suffering."

The Mother closed her eyes. I shut mine as well. When I opened them again, the sun was blazing directly overhead and I was alone. I lay back and looked up at the blue. Again I experienced that soft, fluffy feeling I'd had while sitting with the Mother in Pine Hills— that sense of floating on a gentle breeze. I moved slowly to my feet, took a few steps, hesitated, then turned, staring at the spot she had occupied under the tree. My knees folded, collapsing like a marionette's. Kneeling, I placed my palms together, bowed down, and touched my forehead to the earth, remaining there until it felt as if my head had melted into the ground.

I longed to stay by the cave forever, but knew I had better continue looking for base camp. I finished off the last drops of water and was disheartened to find there was no more food—only the Mother's discarded apple. After returning to the cave, I began stuffing my belongings into the day pack when, not more than a few hundred yards down the hill, I spotted the trail. *How did I miss it? Was I was so intent on finding shelter that I couldn't see what lay before me?* I marched down the path, munching on the Mother's leftover apple, figuring it would give me enough energy for the two- or three-hour hike to base camp.

The sun was dipping behind the mountain by the time I reached my campsite. To my surprise, the food net was missing from the tree, and the propane canister was nowhere to be found. *Him again.* Slowly, I stuffed my sleeping bag into its sack and packed up my gear, all the while feeling unusually detached from the bushman's plunder and wondering if this was similar to what the Mother had meant about not clinging to pain. Then I flashed onto her words of more than twenty years before, about the dangers of wild animals and the woods. My job, I decided, was both to see my body as temporary and to take whatever precautions were necessary to guarantee its safety, even if it meant staying on the trail.

With a twinge of vigilance, I stood up, visually combed the area, and listened for signs of further invasion. Finding nothing, I hoisted the pack onto my back and strolled to the car, once again feeling weightless and brimming with love.

Chapter Three

A World Collapsing

S cents of pine, moist rock, and wild animals wafted in and out of my consciousness. Thinking I was still in my cave in the Chiricahuas, I reached out from under the covers to softly pat the coyotes, only to brush my hand up against the fur of my Old English sheepdog mix, whose tail began thumping against my bed. "Delilah, it's you," I crooned. A song sparrow chirped in sliding arpeggios outside my window as I lingered in bed savoring the memory of my quest.

Eventually making my way to the bathroom, I stared at myself in the mirror. I looked the same as I always had—gray-green eyes, brownish hair, impish features that some men found attractive—yet something had changed, lending me a new, more peaceful appearance.

After my morning walk with Delilah, I wandered into the living room, which I rarely used. A large Oriental rug covered the tan wall-to-wall carpeting, and in lieu of furniture, colorful pillows imported from Turkey and India were tossed casually in bunches. I sat at the center of the rug and contemplated two framed prints of Giotto's St. Francis of Assisi hanging on the side wall. I wondered if the wild birds that were said to perch on the good saint's arms foretold the future. Then I gazed into the face of Fra Angelico's

Mary on the end wall, her eyes wide open, hands crossed at her breast, receiving the kneeling angel's message about the coming birth. Delilah nudged my hand with her nose. As I combed my fingers through her bangs, revealing her shiny black eyes, I asked: "Do you know the truth, girl? Did my meeting with the vanishing Mother happen or was it just a dream?" Delilah happily brushed her tail back and forth against the rug.

In the few days before classes resumed I had time to walk, write, and lie in sandy arroyos under palo verde and mesquite trees. The Mother's presence permeated everything. Her garments spread across ridges of the Tucson Mountains, reflecting the pinks of the setting sun. Her hips and breasts undulated in the heat waves rising off the horizon, and her long hair unraveled into winding ravines. The tingling stillness of the desert air spread inside me like a mist, saturating me with fleeting glimpses of a happiness that existed beyond the passing of light into darkness, day into night, life into death.

Then Monday came. I dragged myself to statistics class, but on my way there students' faces jostled my senses. My mind twisted and whirled like a kaleidoscope, rotating fragments of glass into new patterns with each turn. Every step I took gave way to uncertainty; a world was collapsing under my feet. Stopping to rest on a wall, I wondered how to piece together what was real and what wasn't. As sparrows hopped and pecked around me, a classmate suddenly tapped me on the shoulder, urging, "Come on, Luce. It's late."

During the lecture, my thoughts drifted like seedpods on puffs of wind. I reflected on the Mother's gurgling laughter and her words, wondering how I might bring the experience of her into my daily life. I recalled a visit I'd made years before to a Byzantine basilica in Ravenna, Italy, where diffuse light shone through small windows onto earth-tone mosaics embedded in the rounded ceiling. Walking into the dimly lit sanctuary and feeling my body separate into sunlit particles was something I could never explain. To describe the sensation, I used terms like "mystical," "suspended in space," and "timeless," none of which gave full flavor to the experience. What was it about that small, dark temple on the Adriatic Sea that made it shimmer with other-worldliness? Could I create a similar feeling in my own living room?

At last, the professor's droning had stopped and students were preparing to leave. My friend Diana laughed. "Are you going to sit here and think about statistics for a while?"

Under the Fra Angelico painting in the living room I decided to fashion an altar filled with items I had collected over the previous few days. As a child, I would spend hours decorating a bookshelf for Christmas, using cotton for snow, a mirror for ice, skating and skiing figurines, and in a far corner a manger with Jesus, Mary, Joseph, and all the shepherds and animals. Now, in much the same spirit, I began covering cement blocks with maroon burlap, then placed a slab of flagstone across the top. Over the flagstone I arranged a Middle Eastern weaving salvaged from a yard sale, and on top of that I set the poster of the coyote.

For a long time I stared at the poster, struck by the similarities between this creature and the wolf from my childhood. To me, the wolf had meant freedom, excitement, living in the wild, unencumbered by interruptions from adults— especially my mother, who was forever fearful of my well-being. Why did the Mother appear soon after the wolf? What did the unrestrained independence of the wolf and the playful, unconditional love of the Mother have to do with each other? *Perhaps both these qualities are related to the immortal nectar I'm supposed to find. Things would be so much easier if it were something I could just drink.*

Continuing my creative task, I reached for an oak frame and arranged within it a length of white silk—a place for imagining the Mother. I then lit a candle, placing it to the left of the frame, and set a stick of sandalwood incense aflame to the right of it, poking the unlit end into a piece of volcanic rock. After contemplating the grouping, I scurried outside to select a few stones and branches, and switched items around until the arrangement was just right. My heart swelled. I knelt down, folded my palms together, and touched my forehead to the floor. Smoke from the incense curled around the picture frame, revealing an image of the Mother's face on the cloth, which soon faded to stark white again. Tears welled up in my eyes. *Have I been seeing things all along? How can anything so seemingly real be merely a product of my imagination?*

I sat crumpled, and repeated the only phrase I could remember from the lilting tune I had listened to on my way home from Rainbow Moods Music and Book Store that morning: "Let my spirit fly to you. No place could be too far. Remove this cloud of ignorance and show me where you are . . . and show me where you are."

For days I spent long hours in front of my altar singing, praying, holding my palms together. From time to time I'd step outside to contemplate saguaros, giant beings of the Sonoran Desert, lifting my arms to mirror their supplication to the sky. On a few occasions I crept out into the night to sleep at the foot of the saguaro behind my house, thinking the Mother might come to it under the cover of stars. I'd fix my eyes on its silhouette as I fell asleep, imagining my body stretched toward the heavens. Although I didn't see or hear the Mother on these adventures, I did feel her peace.

On one such morning I awoke and, reaching out of my sleeping bag, touched something cool and leathery. *A rattlesnake!* I rolled away like a tumbleweed, whereupon the serpent flashed its tongue and slithered off. Seeing that its head was narrow, instead of triangular, I knew it was not a rattler but rather a bull snake. Could it be the Mother, I wondered, warning me of the hazards of sleeping unprotected in a desert where snakes, tarantulas, and scorpions crawl in profusion? I slung my sleeping bag over my shoulder, shuffled toward the back gate. Once inside, I soaked in the bathtub, sinking into a dark fog that clouded my vision and struggling over what to do with my life.

"You can't quit when you're nearly finished! So you had an experience in the mountains. Jung had experiences all the time!

Does that mean you have to stop everything?" My advisor, Pat Frost, a boyish-looking woman in her early fifties with short, graying hair, peered at me through thick glasses.

"Sure it sounds crazy, but I don't know what else to do," I said. "Classroom material seems to fill my head with concepts that no longer have meaning to me."

Pat planted her elbows on the desk, rested her chin on folded knuckles. "What happened in the mountains, anyway?"

I opened my mouth to speak, but words failed to emerge, scattered as they were in the chasm separating my experience in the Chiricahuas from the matter-of-fact world of university degrees. I lowered my head. "I don't know how to explain it."

Pat leaned back in her brown vinyl chair and wrapped her hands together behind her head. Enunciating each syllable precisely, she said: "Look, why don't you finish this semester. Enroll for your twelve credits of practicum in the summer. Act *as if* you intend to complete your degree. Just go through the motions."

I rolled and unrolled the course catalog while mentally running through a patchwork of images—the bushman, the coyotes, the cave, the Mother, the inexplicable love. Raising my head, I looked at Pat. "What good would that do?"

"It would give you time to think—and maybe contexts, like Ron's Gestalt class, for processing whatever went on in the mountains."

I swallowed.

She rocked her chair forward. "Why don't you talk to Diana."

I nodded and bit my lower lip. Diana had been a divinity student before coming to the counseling department. Maybe she would have some insights beyond the realm of psychology.

"You'd make a good therapist, Luce. The experience you had might make you an even better one. Give yourself time."

I looked up and smiled. "Okay, I'll try. Thanks."

I stepped out into the smoldering air and hurried down the cement pathways adjoining the clusters of four-story brick buildings. My mind spun like a hamster on a wheel, sending notions of right and wrong tumbling every which way. Nearly stumbling on a curb, I had to grab a tree branch to keep my balance. At last tossing my purse and papers in the car, I sat behind the wheel contemplating an upcoming haircut appointment that now seemed meaningless. I scrutinized myself in the rearview mirror. *I need it, though. I look just like my dog.*

After my trim, I lingered in front of a pet store and then slipped inside. Parakeets chortled and terriers yipped incessantly. A red Siberian husky, too large for its cage, chased itself in circles, biting at its right hind foot. I was amused at the husky's inventive way of entertaining himself under such inhumane circumstances. At the other end of the stacked rows of cages was a gray-and-white malamute, lying quietly, its hollow blue eyes staring into space.

"How much is that red husky?" I asked the sales clerk.

"Ma'am, he's marked down from five hundred dollars to four hundred twenty-five."

My heart beat fast. *Oh gosh, what am I getting myself into? I'll know I'm crazy if I pay that much for a dog.* I felt as though I were on a conveyor belt with no possibility of turning back. "Can I see him?"

The clerk left me alone with the puppy in a tiny, bare room. When I tried to pick him up, he twisted his body and threw his head from side to side. Then he paused long enough for me to see that he had yellow eyes. The way they darted about, not seeming to register the world around him, suggested that he was a victim of pet store abuse. Right away I wanted to rescue him and reintroduce him to freedom.

I carried the writhing beast to the counter. "Do you take credit cards?"

With the puppy straining and shaking his head against the leash I'd tied to the window knob, I drove north down Oracle and turned onto Ina, past the flat-roofed, single-story brick homes nestled against desert landscaping. At the cul-de-sac, I pulled into the carport of my adobe rental, tucked the little husky under my arm, its gangling legs flailing, and set him down in the ocotillo-fenced yard. "I'll be right back, little fellow."

Delilah greeted me at the back door, sniffing me all over. "You know something's up, don't you, girl?" I said gently. Once inside, I stared out the sliding glass door to Mount Lemmon, guardian of the Catalina range. Delilah pawed at my leg, pleading with me to take her out. "Poochie, we have a new puppy. How would you like to be his mom?"

After introducing the dogs, I dragged the phone cord to the sliding glass door, where I could watch the animals' getting-to-know-you antics, and called Diana. "Guess what I got?"

"What do you have, Luce?" Diana asked in her faint Texas drawl.

The puppy dashed around and around nipping at Delilah's legs. She growled, bounded at him, and knocked him over. "A red Siberian husky. His name is Shaman of Wands."

"Oh my God. What craziness prompted you to do that?"

I stuttered as I watched my usually peaceful sheepdog pummel the little husky into the sand over and over again until he whimpered and lay quietly looking up at her. "That's what I need to talk to you about. Something happened to me while I was in the Chiricahuas over break."

"I've wondered about you lately. Is everything okay?"

"Well, not really. Can we have lunch after Pat's class? Somewhere quiet?"

Diana was tall, nearly six feet, and slender like a fashion model. Clothes draped over her body as if she had planned every fold. Her brown eyes, behind large yet delicate horn-rimmed glasses, were soft, doelike. She sat leaning against a tree with her long arms wrapped around her knees. "That's a pretty amazing story, Luce— kind of like St. Anthony in the desert! Speaking of which, you said the coyotes and the woman appeared early in the morning, when you hadn't had anything to eat or drink for a while. Is there any possibility it was a dream or vision?"

We both laughed, but even so I could feel myself knotting up inside. I pinched my sandwich and with the other hand clasped my shoulder as if to hold myself together. "That's what I don't know. It was pretty real. At first, I was okay with the Mother gone because I could still feel her everywhere; now, I'm having some weird problems. Dizziness, forgetting where I am, strange dreams. The other day in the cafeteria I thought my head would burst from the clinking of glasses and plates as a busboy cleared a nearby table. Sometimes I feel deep peace, too, but that's dwindling. I don't know what to do."

Diana reached over to touch my knee, then slipped her hand into mine. "Luce, believe me. If something like that happened to me, it would change my life, too."

My eyes stung with tears. Taking a deep breath, I let my hand fall to my lap. Then I leaned back and took another bite of my sandwich. "Pat says I should continue with my course work to give myself time to think."

"Does that feel okay to you?" Diana asked while pouring coffee from her thermos.

I stared at the Catalina Mountains, recalling the panoramic view from my cave in the Chiricahuas. "One part of me sees the practicality in it. The other part wants to take off, wander the world, find another cave where the Mother would come to me. Maybe in Hawaii. I've heard there are *lots* of caves on the Big Island."

Diana placed her hand on my shoulder and studied me with a deep tenderness. "Luce, didn't the Mother herself say you would have to cross some hurdles?"

I fished an apple out of my brown bag and examined it. "Yes, she did."

"Maybe this is all part of it." Diana's full mouth smiled, forming faint dimples at the corners.

Taking a bite of the apple, I said, "I guess we'd better go to class. I feel a little better now that we've talked, but I still don't know exactly what to do."

We got up and sauntered arm in arm to the counseling building, arriving just in time for Transactional Analysis.

After class, Diana squeezed my hand. "See you at Ron's next week. Maybe you'll be inspired to take the 'hot seat.'"

"Yeah, maybe it's time," I said.

Several nights later I woke up past midnight in a cold sweat. A man with a pistol had been chasing me down alleyways, over fences, into warehouses. I switched on the light, rested my eyes on a pastel painting. *Oh, Mother, please help me.* I sighed and dropped my head to the pillow, leaving the light on as I drifted back to sleep.

Over breakfast I mapped out an early morning hike the dogs and I could take along the Pima Canyon Trail. But did the nightmare portend a repeat of my chase in the Chiricahuas? I wondered. If so, was I to entrust myself to fate and not worry about my future, as the Mother had advised? Because Delilah was too friendly and Shaman too young to offer much protection, I added my hunting knife to the food and supplies about to go in my day pack.

The dogs and I meandered over a knoll of reddish shale before descending into the canyon, where we hiked beside a lush stream lined with seep willows, wolfberry bushes, and cottonwoods. Shaman flopped along, biting at Delilah's hind legs until she paused, wheeled around, and let loose a sharp bark at him. Her ears snapped up like a jack-in-the-box, then dropped down again just as fast, punctuating her disciplinary act. Shaman rolled over on his back, his tongue hanging out the side of his mouth. No longer did his eyes dart around mindlessly, as they had when he first came home from the pet store. *Thank God for that.*

At a spot where the stream formed a shallow pond, the dogs stopped for a drink and I squatted in the sand. Several groups of people passed by in both directions. The *lap-lap* of the dogs' tongues echoed in my ears and began circulating through my head in surging waves. My body proceeded to vibrate in response to an urgent pulsing of blood. The temperature was nearly ninety degrees, yet I couldn't stop my teeth from chattering. I felt strange—hot and cold all at once. I pulled off my boots to cool my feet in the stream, but sounds and sensations stalked me. *Maybe I need to eat.* "Come on, Delilah, Shaman. Let's sit over here." I crawled up an incline to a cottonwood. There I ripped open my sack and devoured some of my sandwich.

The shaking persisted. *Maybe I'm just scared. But why?* My eyes darted up the trail, back down, then up the ravines on both sides of the canyon. I saw nothing but casual hikers chatting, or stopping to gaze through binoculars at birds. Their voices, the rustling of leaves in the breeze, and the gushing water all echoed through a hollow inside my brain. Holding my head, I felt a scream rise like a bubbling volcano about to erupt. *I've got to get out of here.* I stuffed everything back into my pack and jumped up. "Come on, Delilah, Shaman."

With the dogs panting behind me, I splashed across the shallow stream and scrambled through wolfberry bushes on the other side of it, thinking I could move faster by avoiding passersby. Up the incline I went, still off the trail, stumbling and even falling before I emerged, emptied and wasted, at the spot where I'd parked my car.

In the mirror at home, my hair and face appeared dusty and caked, like an Aborigine's. *I look like the way I feel.* A bath soothed my aching muscles and smarting scratches. After running cold water over bruises, I sunk down to rest in the hot tub, only to be overcome once again with the strange shivering. *What's happening to me? There's no one pursuing me now but the demons of my own mind!*

I sought solace at my altar, hoping the Mother would relieve me of my mental anguish, but later that night the chase dream returned. I awoke transfixed, pinned to my mattress in a coat of chain mail. In the morning, to alleviate the shaking I rode my bike around the neighborhood, singing loudly to chase away the clanging each little sound was making in my ears. Scorched by the heat, I came home as dusk was falling, then slumped onto the temple-room floor, lit the candle, and hunched down by the altar, shivering.

Certain that I was going mad, I pondered the Mother's words about the soul being the source of true happiness. If that was so, and if my encounters with her were guiding me to this fount of joy, why, then, had my despair increased? Was my trust in the reality of the vanishing Mother causing me to lose my mind? Too frightened to sleep, I sang repeatedly: "Oh, holy Mother, comfort me. Let me hear you once more whisper my name. Lonely and frightened, like dust in the wind, I'm lost in this infinite world."

The sun woke me, shining its beams on the floor, where I lay rolled in a ball. After toast and coffee, a short bicycle ride to Ron's house refreshed me enough to participate in the three-hour group session. Sam, a burly fellow who worked with prisoners, drove up at the same time I did. He grinned broadly beneath his baseball cap, walked briskly toward me, and said in a Brooklyn accent, "Looks like you had a late night." He wrapped his arm around my shoulder as we walked toward the house.

I had always enjoyed Sam's company, but found myself wincing under his touch. "I'm in trouble, Sam. I hope I can 'work' this morning."

"What's wrong? You don't seem to be your usual perky self."

I kept my head down, unable to look at him as I replied. "I don't know. Whatever it is, it feels pretty crazy."

We went through the open door into the small living room where students were gathering in a circle on dining room chairs, couches, and davenports. Ron, a slender man with graying hair, asked, "How many people want to work today?" Six of the twelve raised their hands. Usually the time allowed for three workers, never more than four. Ron stroked his beard, puckered his lips. "Hmm, I guess we'll have to do some negotiating."

Sam said, "Luce really has to work."

I felt heat flash over my face. Wiggling my toes, I looked at Sam, then at Ron.

"Is that true, Luce? You don't take the hot seat very often." Ron paused to look around the circle, then back at me.

I nodded.

"Well, c'mon then. I guess it's your turn," Ron said.

I crawled onto a pillow in front of him.

"So, tell us what's going on," Ron urged.

I talked about the man in the Chiricahuas, my nightmares, and the strange physical sensations I had been experiencing. Discussing them exaggerated the trembling.

Ron uncrossed his legs and leaned forward. "How does your body feel?"

"Shaky." I tried to smile and grasped my elbows to control the shivering. "I think I need to talk to the man who's chasing me."

"Okay. What do you want to call him?"

Ron's voice sounded as if it had come through a stove pipe. I held my jaw stiff to stop my teeth from chattering. "I don't know— 'Chaser.'" I clutched my knees to my chest.

Ron stroked his beard. "Would you like someone to sit next to you while you work? To help you if you need it?"

I nodded and swallowed, licking my parched lips. "Maybe Sam."

Sam tiptoed over in his bare feet and sat close, without touching me.

"When you're ready, when you feel like you can see him clearly, go ahead and tell Chaser how you feel," Ron instructed.

I looked at the empty space in front of me and imagined Chaser sitting there. My mind went blank. *I'd better relax. I'm not going to see him if I try too hard.* Eventually, the man with a pistol from my dream slipped into my brain, causing me to quiver once again. To get past the fear, I knew I had to say something. "I don't like you chasing me," I asserted, glancing at Ron for reassurance.

"Keep looking at Chaser. Tell him what he looks like," said Ron.

Staring at Chaser, my hands shaking, I whispered, "You look dark . . . scary." I bent forward, covering my eyes with my palms.

After a long pause Ron asked, "Tell Chaser who he is for you."

Rocking back and forth, I searched my mind while images of him kept shifting—from figures in childhood nightmares to the man in the Chiricahuas to present-day dream characters. "I don't know. He's awful. His face keeps changing." Then I broke into sobs.

When I had quieted down, Ron said, "If it seems right, ask him who he is."

I could feel my fingers clenching against my palms as I slowly I turned to Chaser. "Who are you?"

Ron pointed for me to move to Chaser's place.

Already familiar with this method of working, I crawled to the pillow in front of me. Something about being in Chaser's seat calmed me. I closed my eyes and waited. All at once I felt an energy that was not my own. Words assembled in my mind, and slowly I spoke them: "I am the faceless dark pursuing you. I am your nightmares, your age-old fears, everything in you that is filled with terror of the unknown."

With that I returned to my pillow, fascinated by the peculiar strength I'd felt while sitting in Chaser's place. Out of the corner of my eye I saw Ron settle onto the back of his chair to watch what I would do next. As I looked at Chaser's seat again, a race down the dark alley of my dreams began to filter into my brain. My limbs started to quiver and again I felt I must run for my life. Folding my arms, I held my stomach and rocked back and forth. "How can I make him go away?"

Ron spoke slowly, deliberately. "Is that what you want?"

"I can't have this thing following me around all my life!"

Leaning forward in his chair and stroking his beard, Ron asked, "Will it work for you to tell him to go?"

I groped inwardly for the strength to order the dark form to leave, but could find no words to express the strange mixture of fear and grandeur I felt. "Every time I think of something to say, it gets lost or seems trite."

"Speak directly to him. See if it works to tell him to go."

I took a deep breath and somehow managed to blurt out, "Stop . . . chasing me." My head swam; the room vanished into a haze. I bent over and rested my head on my knees, breathing hard. I soon felt the tips of Sam's fingers on my back, like a cat stepping gingerly onto fresh snow. As I sank into his touch, he let his palm rest on my spine, warm and strong. I leaned against his chest and felt his arms enfold me. At that point I started crying freely, sucking in quick breaths between the sobs. Finally, I blew out one long sigh, and my body went limp.

Gradually, my courage came back, and I sat upright again.

"Is Chaser still there?" asked Ron.

I nodded.

"What do you want to tell him?"

"Go away," I growled, like an animal. "Stop chasing me."

"Louder," said Ron.

"Stop it."

Ron raised his voice. "Go on. Louder."

"Stop chasing me!" All at once I felt an uncommon strength come over me. *Stop it! Stop it! Stop it!* I shouted again and again. Then I took a deep breath. Sitting tall and straight to savor the energy radiating from my body, I felt my face beaming. "He's gone," I announced.

The room gradually came back into focus, and everyone in it remained still for several minutes. Then Ron asked, "How does your body feel?"

I twisted around to test it out. "The shaking's gone—for the moment, anyway. Emotionally, I'm worn out, and at the same time I feel clear and free."

"Your eyes look really bright." Sam commented.

I looked at his face and touched him on the shoulder. "Thanks."

"What're you going to do for homework?" Ron asked.

"Oh, I don't know—go to a movie, maybe take the long way home on my bike, watch the stars, not think too much, enjoy the comfort I'm feeling right now."

I slipped out of class without staying to chat, and pedaled down quiet streets lined with palo verdes and mesquites. My pores opened wide to receive the warmth. The shaking had eased into a rather pleasant pulsing of life blood throughout my body. Sounds still seemed unusually loud, however, especially the pebbles crackling under my bicycle tires, the *wheet-wheet!* of the cactus wren, the soft whirling of swamp coolers on top of flat-roofed houses. Yet rather than upsetting me, as they had before, they invited me into their chorus, weaving in and out of my brain in musical patterns.

At home, I rested in the chaise lounge on my cement porch, where the ocotillo fence enclosed a sparse plot of sand spotted with creosote bushes and one mesquite tree. A roadrunner pushed through a space in the fence and ran across the sand, grabbing an insect with its beak, then uttering a staccato *eah-eah!* before disappearing again. Delilah and Shaman scratched to come outside, where they played their perpetual game of Shaman pulling Delilah's raglike ears and Delilah giving the husky a tumble. The smell of charcoal and barbecuing chicken mingled with the hot evening breeze while shadows crept up the mountain and slipped into twilight. The sky then shifted its display of pastels into a black-blue, unveiling the Bright Star of the East.

Even though the Gestalt session had brought relief and a new perspective, I felt uneasy about the dark corner of my brain that had given life to the dream stalker. What was the strange voice that claimed to be the source of my fear? Shuddering, I began to suspect that my experience of Chaser was beyond the reach of therapy. *What is the use of therapy for me—or anyone else for that matter?* I dreaded the possibility of sounds shattering my nerves once again, of the shakiness returning, or the nightmares. I was convinced that my only source of solace was the Mother.

Later, at my altar, I lit the candle and gazed at the photograph of the coyote. A throbbing emptiness deadened my heart. Images of the chaser sent fear rippling though my veins. Delilah poked her nose into my hands, then rested her head on my lap. The little husky uttered a soft howl, crouched down, and inched forward to nuzzle between Delilah and me. "Your eyes are just like his. See?" I told Shaman, turning his face toward the coyote poster.

Then I stroked the black dog's bangs. "What's happening to me, Delilah?" Under the mop of hair that made her look like a gentle clown, she rolled her eyes, showing the whites. I stared at the cloth in the oak frame. *Mother, why can't life be simple, like it is for these sweet dogs? I don't know how to do what you said. How can I not be worried about my thoughts or about what happens to me?* I curled up with Delilah and Shaman, and sang, "Down yonder, green valleys where streamlets meander, where twilight is fading, I pensively roam . . ." I repeated the campfire song until I drifted off to sleep.

A light touch on my shoulder and the sound of bubbling laughter woke me in the night. I lurched upright. "You came!" I covered my mouth with my hands, my heart dissolving into the Mother's love. The smell of rose petals drifted through the air as my temple room expanded into a sea of luminescence. The Mother whispered words I couldn't understand, something like "Shi, shi, shi," as she sat down and took me into her arms. She wiped my tears with the filmy white cloth she always wore, saying, "My daughter, my daughter."

I clasped my arms around her torso, buried my head in her round belly, curled up like a baby bear against its mother. "I don't know what to do."

As the Mother stroked my back, my thoughts melted like icicles in the warmth of a long-awaited spring day. Then she lifted me into a seated position, and I looked deep into her eyes as they penetrated beyond the darkness of the night sky. My lower lip quivered.

"What's wrong, child?"

"What am I going to do? I can't study counseling anymore."

The Mother stroked my arm and chuckled. "Child, you must finish your training without giving thought to the future or the difficulties it may present."

"You're all that matters to me. Isn't there a place where I can be with you forever?"

The Mother's body rippled with giggling. She smiled and rubbed my chest. "Child, you are here for a purpose. You must do the task you came to earth to do. Only in that way can you come to me."

I looked down and fiddled with my bare feet. "Counseling no longer means anything to me."

"A mother doesn't stop nursing her baby because she has lost interest. Suckling is her job, and so she does it with love and devotion until the child is ready to eat on its own. Even after that, she cooks and cares for the child until it is grown. Counseling is the gift you were created to do at this time. You mustn't stop your schooling just because you are disheartened."

I looked at her. "How can anyone but you help people?"

"Just as your professor helped you today, so will you do the same for others. Every living thing serves the world in its own special way. That is the nature of creation. Trees give fruit, cows offer milk, bees make honey, rivers supply water, and the sun provides light. Everything on earth has a purpose."

"But, Mother, is counseling the only way for me to be useful?"

"For now that is your task. Yet you must always remember not to have concern for the outcome. If you worry about the results of your work, or get too enmeshed in people's problems, you may cause harm to yourself and others. You must recognize that it is not *you* who does the work, but rather the divine nectar moving through you. Therefore, make no claims to your successes or failures. Try to see yourself as only one of many colors in a rainbow."

I hung my head.

"Daughter, just imagine that your clients are me. When you show them kindness and understanding, know that you are doing it for me."

"That would be silly, Mother. How could you ever need my help?"

There was a long silence. The Mother looked at me, her eyes a bottomless well reflecting millions of drowning souls crying to be saved. "I am in everyone who will come to you. By serving them, you will also serve me." She put her hands to her chest, then reached out with palms up, singing in a language I could not understand. When she finished, she wiped her moist cheeks and put her hands together in prayer. "Child, as you perform your tasks, remember that you are no different from the street cleaner who shovels garbage from the gutters, or the vagabond who picks through that garbage for sustenance. To me, all are equal."

The Mother closed her eyes and I closed mine. Reflecting on her description of the divine nectar, I realized she'd given me a clue to its meaning: it was intangible, like a spirit that would enter into me. *Perhaps I am tasting that nectar now, in her presence.* Then my mind went blank, forming a measureless screen on which I floated in infinite space. Lights from a vast milky labyrinth seemed to envelop my head, then my torso, arms, legs, and hands, until I was coated in a womblike warmth. I opened my eyes. Delilah was nudging her wet nose into my palm. The room flickered with the gentle glow of dawn.

Chapter Four

Inextricably Entwined

S am was waiting outside the door to the Blue Willow Restaurant
when I pulled into the parking lot. He had left his baseball cap
behind, but wore his usual baggy pants.

"You look radiant," he said.

"Oh, thanks. It's not my doing. Whatever causes it comes and
goes without warning." I smiled generously and squirmed.

Sam tried to squeeze the two of us through the doorway at the
same time, but his broad shoulders crowded me out. "Waterman—
six o'clock," he said to the hostess who led us to a patio table beside
a waterfall.

"This is lovely," I exclaimed.

"I thought you'd like it." Sam grinned and pulled a newspaper
from his day pack. "What movie do you want to see? Don't make it
too serious. Remember, we're supposed to have fun. This is part of
your homework for group."

I laughed. "How about *Dances with Wolves?*"

"Yeah? You like stuff like that?"

"More than you would ever imagine."

We ordered dinner and talked casually about school. Several

times he caught me staring at his blue eyes—light and watery, like a lake, in contrast to his dark, curly hair.

In the movie theater Sam cradled me in his arms when I cried, which I did throughout most of the film. When the other viewers had emptied out of the theater, I remained in my seat, frozen in the vision of another time—an era when the harmony of Native American communities was being destroyed. "I hope you don't mind my sitting here like this," I whispered. "I can't move."

Sam cupped my hand in his warm palms. "It's fine."

After a few moments I wiggled my feet, stretched my legs, cast a sideways glance at him, and chuckled. "Okay, I think I'm back in this world again. Let's go."

After returning to the Blue Willow, where we had left my car, Sam said, "Let's do something together again, all right?"

"Sure. But I can't say how predictable I'll be." I slipped out of the car and shut the door.

Sam rolled down the window and yelled, "How about an early hike Saturday? I'll pick you up."

After unlocking my Honda, I stepped in and perched sideways on the edge of the seat. "I've got two dogs. One's a puppy."

"Hey, can't you see? My car's a mess anyway. Seven o'clock?"

I swung my door back and forth. "Okay, see you then."

With Shaman and Delilah packed in the backseat of the Jeep, Sam and I drove west toward the Tucson Mountains—a rocky range of volcanic hills dotted with saguaros and chollas—home to rattlesnakes, lizards, and jack rabbits. After parking, we maneuvered through a sandy wash, passing ironwood trees draped in lavender blossoms, then paused at Picture Rock, where early Native Americans recorded images and stories. Stick figures of humans, deer, mountain sheep, and antelope were etched into the rock to honor the mysteries of the unknown. "Incredible!" Sam exclaimed.

I couldn't speak. My body shivered as echoes of ancient voices mumbled through the breeze. Since my Gestalt session, I had begun to accept and even enjoy the occasional quivering of my limbs and the reverberations inside my head. I'd decided these experiences were somehow related to the vitality the Mother had poured into my life and to my subtle new perceptions of the world around me. I slipped my arm through Sam's and dragged him to sit with me at the base of the giant rock, where we stared in silence at the petroglyphs. Faint beats pulsed through the earth and up inside me, resounding in my chest. I laid my ear on the sand to listen to nature's underworld orchestra harmonize with the *boom-boom* of my heart.

"You can feel them, can't you?" I asked, filled with skeletal memories of the Hohokam men and women who had lived there long before. Faint visions of sun melting ancient skin, of flesh peeling and abandoning sinking bones, filtered into my thoughts.

Sam shrugged his shoulders and pressed his ear against the rock. Then he pointed to one of the figures wielding a bow and arrow. "Maybe not the same way you do, but I can relate to the hunters."

Shaman and Delilah tore through the wash after a rabbit, spraying sand on our faces, then pushed wet noses into our cheeks and necks. Sam rolled over, laughed, and grabbed Shaman, who still didn't understand the language of affection. The husky wriggled free to jump on Delilah and pull her ears. Sam scooted after them on all fours, growling. *He's so gentle and childlike, yet strong and sturdy.* My heart spread like tentacles through my body, tingling, sending messages I wasn't sure I wanted to feel—at least not now.

On the way home we talked about other Native American sites we had visited: Mesa Verde, Pagosa Springs, and Chaco Canyon. Sam walked me to the back door, and leaned his shoulder against the carport wall while I let the dogs in. "Can we do this again sometime?" he asked.

I paused in the open doorway, not sure what to say or what to feel. "Yes, and I'll have you over for dinner someday, too." Surprised at how openly I spoke, I closed the door halfway, nervous about inviting him in. *I can't get involved with him. Not while my life is so uncertain.*

Sam backed away and ambled slowly to his car. "Okay. See you in class."

🍂 🍂 🍂

Diana wandered over to me during our break from Transactional Analysis class, and crouched down with a big grin on her face. "I want to know what's going on between you and Sam. I've been watching—it's not just casual conversation, is it?"

I stuffed a handful of chips into my mouth, looked out the corner of my eyes at her, and pinched up my nose. "Oh God, does it show? We've only been to a movie and on a walk."

Diana plunked down onto the grass, resting on one hand. "He wandered around like a lost puppy after Ron's group. You little stinker, you sneaked out the door without saying good-bye. Just—*poof*—disappeared. He can't take his eyes off you, and you're glittering like a teenager."

"What would a married woman like you know about that?"

"Don't kid yourself."

"Diana, the truth is I don't know what to do." I ran my fingers back and forth over the freshly mowed blades, searching for words to explain my dilemma. "I'm getting more used to my changing inner world, but it's pretty confusing, even shattering at times. My brain sometimes feels like a glass chamber ringing out higher and higher notes, almost to the breaking point." I shook my head, still unable to grasp the reason for my quandary. "Sometimes I wince when he puts his arm around me. Maybe I'm not really ready for a relationship."

"Just start out slow. He's a sweetheart, and I'm sure he's not gonna leave you. But I wouldn't fool around, Luce. You're gonna have to say something."

"Oh God." I emptied the bag of chips into my hand.

Sam waited for me after class, asked how I liked the discussion. I nodded distractedly and took the opportunity to invite him to dinner. "Do you like barbecued fish?"

"Sure." He stood close. I lingered in the gaze of his crystal eyes, then fell away and edged down the hall, picking up my pace as he joined me and walked me to the parking lot.

I was stoking charcoals on my back porch when Sam knocked on the front door. Clutching a bottle of wine, he gave me a hug. I paused briefly in his tender embrace, then twisted away to examine the gift. "White wine. Goes well with fish. Thanks, Sam."

He stared at the temple room, stepped inside.

"I don't wear shoes in there," I said.

He pulled off his sneakers without undoing the laces, tossed them in the entryway, and stuffed his hands in his pockets.

"I'll tell you more about it later." I pulled his left hand out of his pocket and drew him into the kitchen. Vegetables were lined up on skewers. Salmon fillets floated in marinade. The smell of baked potatoes filled the air. Sam followed me back and forth while I carried the food and place settings to the porch. "Come on, Delilah, Shaman. This stuff is too tempting for you." I slid the door open and shoved the dogs inside.

After dinner we sat silently, watching the glow of the sunset reflected on the Catalina Mountains. "Do you want dessert now or later?" I asked.

"Later. I'm curious about the mystery of the barefoot room."

I rose to clear dishes, feeling nervous about broaching the subject I needed to discuss. *I've invited him to dinner and he doesn't know why.*

"What do you want me to do with these?" He wore a frown and dangled an empty serving dish between each thumb and forefinger.

I laughed, my heart warming at the way he held the plates. "Just drop them in the sink. You can help wash another time."

In the temple room I threw down two pillows, and lit the candle. "Shaman, if you can't keep still, you're going outside. Okay?" Shaman followed Delilah's example and lied down quietly, his head resting on one of the pillows. "We'll see how long that lasts," I said.

I invited Sam to sit, slid into a cross-legged position opposite him, and gazed at the altar for a few minutes. It was time to tell him about my meetings with the Mother, and I decided to start at the beginning, when I was five years old. Sam remained silent as I spoke. When I finished, I looked at the floor for a while and then searched Sam's eyes for a response. "So that's what happened, including her most recent appearance. I sit here a lot and talk to her."

"It's beautiful," he said.

"What?"

"Your face glows when you talk about her."

I pulled my knees to my chest and rested my chin on them. "Sam, you're making it difficult to tell you what I have to say."

"What do you mean?"

"Well, I had no idea that you would understand this at all."

He folded his arms across his broad chest. "I don't know if I understand it. In fact I'm sure I don't, but I see the beautiful effect it has on you. What can I say?"

"Do you believe me, Sam?"

"Who am I to say what's real and what isn't? Anyway, what difference does it make if I believe you or not?"

I hesitated, fiddled with the tassels on the pillow. "Sam, it's why I can't have a relationship with you—at least not a normal boy-girl relationship. It's too much for me right now."

He stretched out his legs, leaned back on his hands. "I'm not in a hurry."

I looked up at him and inched closer, tears filling my eyes. "You're not?"

"I'm not saying I don't want it; I'm saying it's okay to go slow. That's what you'd like, isn't it?"

My whole body melted, my eyes opened wide like the full moon. I nodded.

He stood up and paced the floor. "So, what's for dessert?"

Over the next few weeks, we hiked together, studied together, and went to dinner and to movies. Although I wasn't ready to make a commitment, there was no doubt in my mind that Sam and I were somehow inextricably entwined, bound together by an invisible force, perhaps even fulfilling an arrangement sealed on parchment long, long ago. Never in my life had I felt so deeply understood by another human being, and so utterly comfortable.

He was patient with both my stalker-nightmare anxieties and my bouts of fragility. My only concern was his refusal to discuss issues that bothered him at the prison, although I trusted that someday he would feel safe enough to share them. In response to his unconditional acceptance of me, my feelings deepened to such an extent it was hard to imagine life without him. Sometimes I would wake in the night shivering with the fear of losing him, even calling out his name. On these occasions I would wander into the temple room, light a candle, and seek solace in prayer to the Mother.

In Pat's office during the first week of summer session, I produced a draft for a newspaper ad I had written to start a therapy group in the fall, after graduation. I could tell Pat was pleased I'd done some thinking about my career. With a slight glimmer in her eyes, she leaned back in her chair and folded her hands behind her head as she listened to me read the copy: "How do childhood fantasies and dreams affect your life? Group therapy with a Gestalt emphasis."

When I finished, Pat leaned forward, elbows on her desk. "Luce, we've talked about this in class. Most graduates work for an organization a few years before trying to develop a private practice. Even then, many don't make it."

I stuck my chin out, looked steadily into her eyes. "It's the way I want to work. I'm not seeking clients with serious mental problems. I simply want to help people improve the quality of their lives by incorporating some of the ideas sparked by my experience in the Chiricahuas."

Pat smiled. "No matter how good you are, Luce, you're inexperienced. You won't know what sorts of problems clients will bring to your group, even after screening them. Your plan is fine, but who's going to supervise you?"

"I was hoping you would."

Pat rested her chin on her knuckles. "I suppose that's a possibility. Diana has made the same request. Maybe the two of you could come in together."

At the end of August, in the midst of Tucson's muggy monsoon season, Sam and I completed our master's degrees. I received a congratulatory phone call and a generous check from my mother. Other than that, no ceremony punctuated our achievement except for a night out together at the Blue Willow. We sat at our table beside the waterfall. Sam ordered broiled chicken and I asked for baked salmon. Bouncing against the back of my seat, I said, "I'm so excited about having my own clients. I can't wait to use the Mother's advice with them. Remember how she said I would ease her suffering by helping others?"

He rubbed his knee against mine, said, "Umm," and smiled a little half grin. "Maybe my prison job will get better now, too." Thrilled to hear him mention his job, I rested my hand on his. The twinkle in his eye let me know he felt acknowledged.

He immediately set his elbows on the table and rested his chin on his hands. "So, how was your last interview—the one with that guy who dragged his feet about joining your group?"

"God, that's another story. He didn't seem quite right, but for some reason I encouraged him to come anyway."

Sam reached into the bread basket, peeled off a piece of crust, and bit into it. "I thought you're supposed to screen the weird ones out."

In mid-September, under a full moon, I led four men and eight women into the desert behind my house—among them, Miriam, a social worker; Ariadne, an artist; and Ben, a blond fellow in his late twenties still searching for his "life purpose." They gathered around a fire circle to talk about themselves and what they hoped to gain from the sessions. I kept my eye on Saul, who had slunk along behind the others and chosen a spot slightly apart from them. His shoulders and chest were as slender as a ten-year-old boy's. His slanted green eyes shifted from left to right. His oversized fingers brushed across his delicate-looking forehead like praying mantis

legs, pushing away stiff brown hair. Although ill at ease, I reminded myself that nothing he had told me supported my feelings of discomfort. At the end of the session, while everyone else closed their
eyes to contemplate the stillness of the night, Saul fidgeted. All
the while, coyotes howled in the distance.

Diana and I pulled up simultaneously to Pat's home, where we
were about to have our first bimonthly supervision meeting.
I described Saul. "After people have poured their guts out and it's
his turn to speak, he snickers, drums his fingers on the floor, pushes
back his hair, and says, 'Don't ask *me!* I've never done anything like
this before.' Sometimes I catch him looking at me when someone
else is talking." I was embarrassed to tell Pat and Diana the extent
to which my mind dwelled on Saul, and how desperately I wanted
to help him.

"What did you find out when you interviewed him?" Pat queried.

"Not much. He snickered then too. Said he liked the ad and
needed to understand some things about himself."

"Just wait, Luce. You don't have enough information about
him. And don't get sucked in like you used to when one of your
practicum clients was in great need."

"If you get too enmeshed in people's problems, you may cause
harm to yourself and others." The Mother's words echoed in my brain
as I sat on my back porch watching afternoon storm clouds form in
the distance. I knew I was too concerned about Saul. Something
about him was drawing me in—something I couldn't quite put my
finger on. Thunderheads, wild and black, ballooned across the sky,
clashing with fierce winds. Lightning sent veins flashing. Rain fell in
sheets. Delilah and Shaman crawled under the chaise lounge as the
rumbling drew closer. Gusts slammed doors, shook windowpanes,
jolted my thoughts, hurtling my mind into the pelting rain. Surface

roots of saguaros seized the moment to suck water from the deluge. My thoughts fell limp, soaked in nature's bath. *Mother, is this storm your way of releasing me from pestering thoughts? Why must I constantly be separated from your love and plunged into the darkness of my own heart?*

While driving home from a hike in Sabino Canyon with Sam, I asked, "What's wrong? You're awfully quiet."

He pressed on the gas pedal. "I just need a break."

"Come on, Sam. I know you don't like to discuss what's bothering you at work, but maybe it's time. Otherwise, your silence may put a strain on our friendship."

"Friendship? Is that what this is?"

I remained silent.

He took a deep breath and slowed the car. "Okay. I'm trying to get a wilderness survival program started with my prison clients. I may be a city boy, but for a few lucky summers I went to a camp where a counselor taught us stuff you wouldn't believe. When I wasn't so busy, I used to go into the woods with no food, no matches, nothing except the clothes on my back and a hunting knife. I'd stay out for a few days— once for a couple of months. That's why I thought your story was beautiful, and why I got excited after you cried at that movie we went to."

I slipped my hand into his thick palm. "I didn't know you'd gotten excited about that."

Sam looked at me, his blue eyes wide like a young child's. "Anyway, the administration's putting me through hoops about it. Prison life's a brick wall for these guys. There are glimmers of light and then—*bang*—the doors clang shut. My clients are in cages. How can you heal in an iron cage? Most of them have problems like you and me, only much worse. They've been brought up in hell, made angry choices, and ended up in a worse hell. Nature heals me, so I figure it can heal them, especially the wilderness. That's why I'm putting up with this stupid red tape, master's degree included."

Warm, watery impulses ran through my body like rivulets. "Sam, you're full of surprises."

Everyone in our group had taken the hot seat with the exception of Saul. Thoughts of him crept through my mind like ants crawling in underground tunnels. Why doesn't he share? How can I help him be less fearful? Is fear the problem? It was late October when the group members bundled into jackets and stocking caps to cluster around the fire circle for a midsession gathering. They had prepared stories about encounters with invisible friends, wild animals, spirits, and angels, or other nonordinary childhood experiences. No one shuffled a foot during the renderings.

When Saul cleared his throat to speak, the others stared open mouthed. "I have something to tell." His face paled and he looked at me.

I could feel my fingers clutching my legs. "Go on. It's okay."

He cleared his throat again.

Goose bumps rose on my arms. "Go on."

Saul stroked his face, then held one huge hand near his neck, as if to coax out his voice. "When I was five years old, I had dreams about a really ugly beast. I'd wake up shivering, afraid to call out, because my folks beat me each time I made noise in the night. Once, I jumped up from the dream and saw the creature standing there in the dark, with a green glow around it. I was so scared, I peed in my pajamas. The thing had a humanlike head with horns, a three-pronged tip to its tail, claws for fingers. I crouched against the headboard shaking. Then the thing sat on my bed, smiled, and stroked my face, humming a grating, dissonant tune while I held tightly to my pillow. Soon it started to speak, with the same hoarse tones. It coached me in how to get back at my mother and father for the mean ways in which they'd been treating me. That first night my instructions were never to tell my parents anything important and to talk very little."

At supervision I shared what Saul had said.

"Did you find out any more?" Pat asked.

"No. There was no commentary that night, just listening.

I'm at a loss, Pat. I feel almost morbidly sorry for him and can't get him off my mind."

Pat rested her elbow on the arm of her chair and cupped her chin in her palm. "Hmm, his case is complicated. Don't push him."

"Otherwise, you might have an exorcism on your hands," Diana added.

"Great," I said, shivering at the thought. "But worse than all that is what's going on with me. How do I stop thinking about him so much?"

"If it continues, we'll have to look at what he's bringing up for you," said Pat.

I took a deep breath, afraid to uncover exactly what Saul signified to me. "Okay."

I fumbled through the door with packs and dogs, then climbed into Sam's four-wheel drive, already loaded up with food, tarps, cooking utensils, and sleeping bags. We drove up Mount Lemmon the back way, along the dirt road. Later in the day, Sam showed me how to make a lean-to out of branches and sticks, and insulate it with leaves, moss, and pine needles. While hiking, he picked up scat, pulling apart the wild animal feces to identify jawbones, fur, and berry seeds. He taught me how to walk through the woods without making a sound, rolling my foot on the outside from heel to toe. Then he cooked dinner over hot rocks in a small pit, sandwiching lamb chops, lima beans, and corn cobs between grasses and bark. He completed the preparations by shoveling dirt on the underground oven, to keep it covered until the food was cooked.

Sam leaned on the shovel. "I love being out here with you. You're so strong and agile with those beautiful legs."

I laughed. "You're supposed to be digging, not looking at me." With his shirt off he looked like Poseidon, but I was too shy to comment on it.

That night before entering our respective lean-tos, we bundled up in sleeping bags under the open sky to gaze at the stars. Sam nuzzled against me and gave me a lingering kiss on my cheek. His warmth and gentleness entered into me as if we were one. At that moment I couldn't understand my insistence on keeping our distance.

In the morning I crept out of my shelter and, guided by the light of the waning moon, propped myself against a tree to watch the sunrise. Still wrapped in my down bag, I couldn't help but marvel at the unusually red glow lighting the thin clouds overhead. Still, my mind festered. I envisioned Saul's lupine eyes, his long, sinewy fingers. His snickering reverberated inside my head. *How do I get so sucked in when it comes to him?* An invisible drill bit bored into my chest, digging and probing, causing a nagging ache in my heart. The Mother had said, "Child, just imagine that your clients are me. It is not you who does the work, but rather the divine nectar moving through you." Tears moistened the collar of my sleeping bag. *Oh, Mother, how did my mind get so tormented?*

At supervision I announced that I'd taken on my first private client.

"Congratulations, Luce," Diana replied. "But I've been curious about Saul. Did he take the hot seat after sharing that dream?"

"No. As Pat predicted, he probably felt too unsafe to go further. But Miriam, in an irritated tone of voice, asked Saul why he never took the hot seat. He told her that he didn't plan to make a fool of himself by talking to an empty pillow."

"Did you help her out?" asked Pat.

"What do you mean?"

"I don't blame her for being annoyed."

I hemmed and hawed. "I was trying to support both of them. I said he wasn't obligated to work." My stomach churned. *I'm still afraid to tell them how deranged my mind has become over this fellow.*

"You might have asked her how that felt. She went out on a limb to speak up. You don't have to protect him, and you have an obligation to the others to stay with their feelings."

I bent forward, leaned on my knees, and bit my lip. "Miriam's face

turned red when he answered her, then she walked out of group without staying behind to chat, as she usually does. Oh gosh, what'll I do?"

"Practice, Luce. That's why you're in supervision." Pat smiled,
leaned back in her chair, and put her hands behind her head.

In my temple room I lay on my back and over and over again
sang a stanza from my favorite tape: "I am a prisoner of doubt and
of fear, bound like a slave on a boat I cannot steer. How long must
I sail on this sea of confusion before you will carry me ashore?"

Suddenly, Saul's eyes flashed in my mind. I was struck by their
resemblance to the wolf's eyes, and the coyote's, and Shaman's.
I couldn't figure out why I hadn't noticed the similarity before. Did
Saul represent some wildness in me that I was yearning to set free?
The idea seemed a bit farfetched, yet it left my mind feeling light and
open. *Maybe this partly explains my desperation to help him, to liberate
him from the imprisonment so evident in his behavior.*

At the end of group the following week, Saul skulked in the
corner, cupping his chin in his large, smooth hand. He hunched
when he sat, although well-developed legs had him standing over
six feet tall. After everyone left he sidled in close, asked if he could
talk for a few minutes.

What am I going to do? I can't refuse. I slid one foot back. "Sure,
Saul, what's on your mind?"

He snickered. "Oh, I thought it was time to tell you that I've
got some guilt about something I did when I was nine years old.
Remember the creature that came to me in the night? Well, I'd
been accepting counsel from it for a long time, learning how to
make things happen—you know, like making others trip and fall, or
get stomachaches. I was heated up about a beating my mother had
given me. All I'd done was forget to close the lid on the piano after
practicing. That afternoon we drove to the beach. All the way to

the shore I wished she would drown." Saul's green eyes pierced mine. "And she did."

I stepped toward him, withholding an urge to take him in my arms. "Oh, Saul. I'm so sorry. Why didn't you ever tell us this before? What did you do?"

"I closed myself in my room for days. The creature abandoned me, so I thought I'd better pray to God. And I did."

My mind, sucked down into a dark tunnel, flashed on scenes from my own childhood—my father trying to "think" people into doing things, getting angry, threatening to go out drinking if my mother didn't respond to his mental commands. "I'm sure you didn't cause her to drown, Saul. That can't be so."

"Oh yes, I did."

I shuddered, inched toward the entryway, wiped my clammy hands on my skirt. *How am I going to get out of this? I'll focus on his feelings. He came to me with a feeling.* "I know you don't like to talk much in group. But if you could come and work this next week, it would be best. I'm so glad you told me about your feelings of guilt. It must have taken a lot of courage. Will you be all right?" I opened the door to let him out. It took all the willpower I could muster not to grab his hand, sit and talk to him until he felt better. But a primal fear prompted me to let him go.

He slinked out, ducking his head, then turned toward me. "Would you like to go with me to a lecture on witchcraft and necromancy this Friday?"

I sweated in the chilly breeze. My mind swirled into a whirlpool of childhood images: my dad in his youth, beckoning teenage girls to his doorstep with his forefinger; his father, a hell-fire damnation preacher, punishing him for it. I stammered, "We . . . have rules. I can't date or have close friendships with clients."

Saul arched his brows. His face twisted into a grimace.

"Are you sure you're okay?" I stepped toward him.

He disappeared into the dark, his voice strained. "You don't have to worry about me. I'll be just fine."

I dragged myself out of bed in the early morning and meandered through the wash by the dim, emerging light of day. In the middle of the sandy bed I sat cross-legged, wondering about the connection between Saul and my father. Maybe my magnetic attraction to Saul was a disguised urge to know my dad who, I'd heard, was also intense, mysterious, and prone to moody silences.

These musings enthralled me until I was distracted by Shaman, who stood fixated on something in the distance. His white mask framed his yellow eyes, making him look like a wise man painted in ceremonial colors. My husky's otherworldly stare sent my mind into a peaceful swirl that blended past, present, and future into an eternity suspended in a second. Nothing, not even Saul or my absent father, could interrupt this feeling of serenity.

The first rays of sun over the Catalinas brightened into an image of white veils—faint, translucent, slipping in and out of the spectrum of rainbow colors. A red-tailed hawk cried out, *"Cheeeeeee."* I squinted, shaded my eyes with my hand, watching it soar. Then I gazed in awe. The Mother's robes billowed as she slid along a beam of light. Slowly, she drifted down, then alighted on the sand and stood with arms raised overhead. I was dumbfounded, wondering why, under the circumstances, I was deserving of her visit.

In a mellow whisper the Mother said, "Come, child." She took me by the hand and led me down the wash. Delilah and Shaman tagged along behind.

I felt like a nine year old. "I've not been able to control my mind, Mother."

She glided, her feet barely touching the ground. "Yes, child, I know. Controlling the mind is a difficult task. Yet the wandering mind is the cause of most of our sorrows."

I walked briskly, sometimes trotting, to keep up with her. "It's like being at the mercy of the wind. Even the smallest breeze carries me away."

She paused under a desert willow, then we settled into the sand beneath it. "Child, it is the nature of the mind to wander. Not until you know the immortal nectar will you be freed of the mind's grasp. Even great saints were at times distracted by their thoughts. One Indian saint, who was a bit proud, thought he had conquered his mind completely. Then God sent him to the river, only a few yards away, for a glass of water. There the saint met a beautiful woman who needed help carrying a jug of water home to her family. The saint, of course, obliged. When he arrived at the woman's house, the family made arrangements for their wedding. They married and bore children. One day they tried to cross the river during a storm. The saint held onto his wife's clothing to stop her from being washed away by the rising current, but to no avail. He then struggled to balance the children on his shoulders, but as he stepped farther out, the water swelled up over his head. Although he yelled for help and thrashed around trying to rescue the children, but couldn't save them from the raging river. In despair he swam to shore, pulled himself onto the beach, looked up, and lo and behold, there was God smiling, waiting for his glass of water. And so it is for us all. We can become easily distracted and lose track of our purpose."

"What can I do, Mother, to control my mind? If saints have trouble, what hope is there for me?"

Bubbling with laughter, she hugged me. "Even the smallest effort will help you reach the goal. Already you have an altar in your home, where you pray and sing. Now you must also practice meditation. Try to sit with your eyes closed, concentrating on the present moment. Do this for short periods of time in the beginning, then for increasingly longer interludes. To help focus your mind, remain still and concentrate on the inflow and outflow of your breath, always bringing the mind back if it begins to wander.

"When your thoughts stray, think of me. Envision the many times you have felt my presence—under the saguaro, in the wash, on your porch—or seen me in the snow, the desert, the mountains, or your temple room. Let these experiences come alive in your imagination and relish them. Or before you start meditating, make me a pudding out of rice, milk, and honey, then picture me eating and enjoying its sweetness. Do any of these things with love in your heart, child. In this way, your mind will become calm."

The Mother picked up the skeleton of a cholla limb—smooth, round, with little holes where prickles had once been—and handed it to me. "You may add this to your altar to help you remember me. Know, as with all things, I am in it and it is in me."

Intent on remembering the details of her meditation instructions, I failed to fully understand her message. "What can I offer you if I have no pudding?"

She stroked my cheek and giggled. "You can offer me a leaf or a flower."

All of a sudden Delilah barked, leapt up, and dashed through the wash after a rabbit, her paws spewing grains of sand as she flew. Shaman scurried behind her. I jumped up, sprinting after them to put on their leashes. When I returned, the Mother had vanished. I dashed about looking for her, feeling foolish to have rushed away without thinking. Then I saw the cholla branch lying on the ground. I picked it up, cupped it in my hand, and closed my eyes to feel the lingering vibration of her warmth and love.

Shaman scratched at my legs and tugged on the leash. "Okay, we're going." As I shuffled through the sand, I looked up at Mount Lemmon, wondering where the Mother had gone and if she would ever again speak of the immortal nectar.

Chapter Five

A Sideshow
of Magic Spells

It was midnight on Christmas Eve. Sam and I settled into a pew toward the back of the of the church, where pine boughs and poinsettia blossoms delighted my senses. I turned to watch the organist, who was playing a Bach prelude. *Saul! So that's why he has such long, sinewy fingers."*

"I know the organist," I whispered.

"He's unusually good," said Sam.

"I think so, too."

We stood for the choir's processional, "O Come, All Ye Faithful." Next came the Hallelujah Chorus, at which point Saul's head sunk into the turtle shell of his black choir robe. He waved his arms around like a crow flapping its wings. He's *directing the choir, too.* He nodded his head up and down, cuing sopranos and basses as he mouthed the lyrics. Then he whirled one hand in the air, twittering the melody with the other, before both hands suddenly crashed down, the massive organ pipes vibrating the belly of the sanctuary. The minister read: "For unto you is born this day in the city of David . . ." A brief sermon was sandwiched between carols. Finally, the recessional, "Joy to the World."

"Look!" I said outside the church. "A white Christmas! I wonder if it's ever happened in Tucson before." Hand in hand, Sam and I shuffled through the drifting snowflakes. Prickly pears, saguaros, and chollas were brightened with designs of white. I skipped ahead, grabbed a wad of snow, and threw it at Sam.

"Okay, you're in big trouble." He scooped up two handfuls and ran after me, hurling them at the back of my neck.

I leapt into the car. He pitched snowballs at my window, then ran around and jumped in. We eased out of the parking lot.

"You kept looking at that guy, the organist," said Sam.

"I was fascinated. I didn't know he did this kind of work."

"Where do you know him from?"

"I can't talk about it."

"Oh, a client, huh?"

At home I turned on the Christmas lights strung around the live tree decorated with hand-painted wooden angels. I heated up home-made deep-dish berry pie, smothered pieces with vanilla ice cream, filled glasses with Riesling, and served it all on a wooden tray on the floor in front of the fireplace. Sam and I gazed into each other's eyes, sucking, smacking, giggling, letting the dessert linger in our mouths.

"This love affair is like some ancient Chinese ritual that goes on and on," he said. "It starts with a view of only the ankles for several years, then moves on to the wrists, and finally the eyes, staying with the eyes forever and ever."

"Why Chinese?" I slid ice cream into my mouth and licked the spoon.

"Because I know nothing about them and I also know nothing about this," he replied, vigorously stirring the remains in his nearly empty dish. Then he slurped the last bite and leapt to his feet. "I don't know," he said, holding his wine glass above his head and gesturing with his spoon. "Maybe it's Micronesian, or Mongolian. It's not Brooklyn. I know it's not like this anywhere in Brooklyn." He placed the wine glass under a napkin and pretended to stomp on it, raising his voice like an announcer at a baseball game. "In Brooklyn we break the glass, grab the bride, and drag her away."

My stomach warmed with laughter as I watched his face shining in the firelight. "I've been to a couple of those weddings," I said.

He laid down on the floor and looked into my eyes. "The strange thing is, I like the way we're doing it. At least for now."

Our eyes were two streams at a swirling confluence.

"Me too," I said, too mute to describe the uncharted waters of love that pulsed through me.

I took his hand and pulled him closer. The mere touch of his body against mine brought a sensation of soaring like an eagle. We lay propped on pillows, hands entwined, watching the fire. The flames twisted, crackled, danced in blues, yellows, oranges, and whites. The blaze caressed and curled, winding and sizzling onto loosened bark. Logs sloughed into one another, puffed onto the ashes, heaving, sighing, then a new burst of flame sparkled, ignited by the red coals.

Sam reached for his bowl, nuzzling the back of my neck. "Do you have any more of this stuff?"

Returning from the kitchen, I said, "Look! It's getting light outside. Let's take the dogs for a walk before the snow melts." I knelt behind Sam, slipped him his bowl, and held him around the waist, resting my cheek against his back while he ate.

Before New Year's I held a holiday part for the therapy group. Saul hung in the corner like a jackal. Miriam, Ariadne, and I stood next to the Christmas tree discussing the new direction our therapy sessions would take, an idea I had presented at the previous meeting.

Miriam fluffed her graying hair and fingered one of the Christmas ornaments. "I like the idea of starting the group with a short meditation."

"Just a second," I interrupted. "Let me find out what Saul wants." I motioned for him to come talk now rather than later, after everyone else had left.

He padded over, snickering, eyes darting to and fro. "I saw you on Christmas Eve."

I looked down and felt a flush cross my face. "Saul plays organ," I explained to the group. "Quite well, in fact."

Saul managed a wry smile and steadied his gaze into my eyes. "I'm glad you thought so."

I was finishing my conversation with Ariadne and Miriam when Saul edged in closer. "I'm not going to continue with the group," he announced.

I held back a sigh of relief. *Thank God I won't have to deal with him anymore.* "Don't forget our group contract—that you have to attend two more sessions before stopping."

"Don't worry, I'll be there." Saul folded his hands and drummed his fingers against his knuckles. "By any chance, are you interested in psychic stuff—you know, spirit realm?"

A chill ran through me. I shivered, then glanced at Ariadne and Miriam. For years I had been picking up occult books here and there—material on the Rosicrucians, palmistry, witchcraft—and wanting to meet someone who could teach me more about these subjects. "Yes, I am. Why?"

"Well." He giggled and cleared his throat. "I know some people. Antonio's from Peru, a *curandero* descended from Incas. His wife Sibyl is part Filipina, born in Louisiana. They have a small community in Avra Valley, on the other side of the Tucson Mountains. Sibyl needs a place closer to town to teach her dream classes. Antonio hardly goes anywhere—at least not in his physical body." Saul cackled, his eyes, staring into mine, seeming to carry a secret. "Anyway, I thought maybe you'd let her use this space."

Burning with uneasy fascination, I turned to look at my altar, then at Miriam and Ariadne.

Ariadne beamed, her hazel eyes flashing. "I'd join a dream class if there was a good one."

Miriam nodded vigorously, eyebrows raised. "So would I."

I didn't want to pass up the opportunity even if it did mean more dealings with Saul. Besides, I wouldn't be responsible for him with Sibyl leading the group. "I'd first have to meet her," I said.

Saul's eyebrows looked more pointed than usual, and one side of his mouth curled into a smile. "When can I bring her over?"

I stalled, pausing to look at my watch, all the while trying to figure out if I I'd be able to maintain a professional distance from him in a dream class. "How about Saturday, three o'clock?"

Sibyl had a round face with dark rings circling her eyes, like a gypsy. As soon as she stepped inside, she lit up and swished around the room, her plump body jiggling under her red squaw skirt and peasant blouse. In a high-pitched, almost adolescent voice, she oozed enthusiasm, then paused in front of my altar. "I see you have a destiny with the goddess. Hmm, mmm-mmm. She wears white, doesn't she?"

My face flushed, and my heart skipped a beat. I was magnetized to her, embarrassed at how quickly she had won me over. Yet something warned me to stay casual. I motioned for her and Saul to come into the family room. "Would you like some tea?" I turned, tripping on the edge of the rug. Feeling my face go red, I hurried toward the kitchen.

We settled into chairs at the round dining room table. Sibyl twisted her black braids around her fingers and spoke, stuttering a little humming sound between sentences. "I first met my husband in a dream. He was the seer for an Inca ruler and I was a temple virgin— forbidden fruit. One day after I had strayed outside the temple walls to pick flowers, Antonio wandered by. Our eyes caught and we immediately fell in love. After that we met secretly, and later escaped through a labyrinth of underground tunnels to the sea. In this life our paths crossed during a midnight ceremony at Chichén Itzá, the best-known of all ancient Maya ruins in the Yucatán. He paused midstride in his equinox dance, stared at me with these cat eyes. I spirited him out of Mexico and into America. We knew our destiny was to come to Arizona to teach. We'd seen it in dreams."

Saul snickered and cleared his throat. "If you think *this* is interesting, wait till she starts teaching."

My mind danced to know more about this woman who practiced magic. Another part of me sounded warning bells and flashed red lights. Instead of saying no, however, I found myself proposing, "We could do a trade—you use this space and I take your class for free."

"Luce, what are you getting yourself into now?" Diana asked with a slight frown after I'd told her about my meeting with Sibyl. We were sitting across from each other over lunch at the Good Earth Restaurant.

"She's a gifted psychic, though I'm a little suspicious of her magician husband." I grabbed a slice of hot bread out of the basket and buttered it. "The main drawback is that Saul will still be hovering around. Something about his long white fingers and their incessant drumming haunts me. I often catch him staring at me."

"What kind of community is it, Luce?" Diana dabbed her mouth with the edge of her napkin.

I took a bite of my cheese omelet. "What?"

She leaned toward me and enunciated, "That Peruvian couple—what kind of community are they running?"

I'd been so enamored of Sibyl that I'd failed to obtain this important piece of information. "I didn't think to ask," I replied sheepishly.

Diana sipped her coffee. "You mean you opened the doors to your home on the recommendation of a man whose credentials are dubious at best, after listening to what amounts to a fairy tale? I have to tell you quite frankly, Luce—I'm worried."

I wrinkled my nose, stretched my mouth over to one side. "We all know I'm a sucker for fairy tales. Do you really think I'm in trouble?"

On my way home from lunch, I began to think Diana's concerns might be justified. For one thing, perhaps I *would* have problems dealing with Saul in the dream class. Even so, I decided, because of his artistic nature, his peculiar twists of mind, and his preoccupation with magic, he had the potential to enlighten me on what lay at the bottom of my father's torment I'd heard so much about from family and friends. Besides, he had brought me a giggling psychic who made my heart sing. Something about her laugh reminded me of the Mother. Yet Diana's warning on this score, too, still rang in my ears. *Here's that what's-real-versus-what's-not question again. How am I to know the answers without proceeding, and at the same time exercising caution—which appears not to be one of my strong suits?*

Upon my return home, Shaman greeted me, lingered in my hug, nuzzling his nose into my neck. "You're all healed from your pet-store trauma, aren't you, boy?" He wagged his tail. Several weeks before, I'd enrolled him in puppy classes, and this seemed a perfect time to take the dogs out to practice the lessons—heeling, sitting, and coming when called. No sooner did we begin our work-out than Delilah lay on her tummy, legs and chin sprawled tightly against the sand so as not to be asked to go through the paces. When we finished, I let Shaman loose to play while I rested under a mesquite tree. There I closed my eyes and focused on the present moment, as instructed. However, images of Sibyl—her giggle, her psychic powers, her Peruvian story—overpowered my best efforts at quieting my mind.

As I opened my eyes, resting them on the top of Mount Lemmon—a reminder of peace and constancy—I wondered how the Mother knew when to appear, since sometimes she came when my hands were not in prayer position. Didn't I need help right now? Hadn't I fallen into an enchanted world of magic spells? I couldn't understand why I would be enraptured by Sibyl and Antonio if they meant to harm me, and why I kept forgetting to ask about their community. Confusion spun me around in the cobwebs of my mind.

A throng of captivated listeners crowded around Sibyl at the first meeting of her dream class. She giggled effervescently. "I can see your husband is having difficulty with one of his coworkers," she said to Coral, a pixie blond from my therapy group. "You'd better be careful of that dark-haired man who's after you at work," the psychic squealed to a woman dressed in red. *Wow! She's really good.* Settling herself on the floor, Sibyl fanned her turquoise squaw skirt around her and waved her hands, inviting us to form a circle. Once we were seat-ed, we each told a dream to which she responded with colorful inter-pretations, all the while jingling the bracelets that adorned her wrists. The air was electrified by her charm.

Even Saul participated. Resting a notebook on his large palms, as if on a lectern, he read: "A woman I like beckons me into the woods, into a grove of trees near a stream. It's a Garden of Eden. We take off our clothes and tickle tender flesh with leaves from willow branches. Then we chase and dance, play hide-and-seek until we fall on the moss covering the warm banks under forgiving willows. We roll over blueberries, smearing our bodies with sweet moisture and drinking the juice."

How can he be so macabre and innocent at the same time?

Sibyl squealed. "Saul! That woman's coming to you. I know she is!"

He snickered and flashed a sideways glance at me. His eyes poured a liquid potion into mine, causing my stomach to writhe. *I sure hope he doesn't imagine it's me in that Garden of Eden.*

Sibyl spun more stories of love and adventure, enlivening each person's dream with enchantment. At some point I slipped into a realm in which neither my thoughts nor my feelings belonged to me. A curtain was being drawn over my senses. Casting away all caution, I leapt into Sibyl's bewitching world.

After class, I fixed tea and sat on the couch to savor the thrill of the evening. My mind flashed to medieval times and stories of witchcraft, spells and charms, owls and bats in woodland cottages, pots boiling with potent mixtures. Then I noticed my message-machine light flashing. I clicked it on to Sam's voice. "Guess what! My proposal's been accepted. I got the go-ahead to take a handful of prisoners on four week-long treks into the wilderness—all guys I've been working with for a couple of years. Can I pick you up tomorrow at five to celebrate?" His voice sounded distant and his words, somehow too ordinary. Then I shook myself to my senses, still aching for Sibyl's enthralling presence.

By spring, the dream class had grown to three groups, Sam had taken two experimental ventures into the mountains, and my practice had increased to eight private clients and a second ongoing therapy gathering. The original group—which had continued intact with the exception of Saul—was opening each session with meditation, to help them enter more deeply into themselves, beyond the usual bounds of therapy. "The way I feel after meditation makes it easier to understand myself while I'm in the hot seat. It helps me see how I block out my love of life," Ariadne stated one evening, her eyes welling with tears.

I had introduced the benefits of meditation by telling the group about my childhood encounter with the Mother, although I refrained from speaking about the more recent episodes, for fear of being misunderstood. "Sometimes I feel the Mother from my childhood vision cradling me, bathing me in her love," I explained. "Before we finish tonight, I want to take you through a guided meditation that might evoke a similar feeling."

All this time, I was only partially aware that Sam was a critical source of grounding for me. During his trips into the mountains, I had begun to assist Sibyl, converse with her about class members, and help her with publicity. At dream gatherings, she had me sit next to her, perhaps to somehow transmit her knowledge to me. There was no formal teaching, only interpretations of our dreams, especially my own sometimes clairvoyant, sometimes bizarre ones. Every once in a while I'd dream that I had learned to mix herbs and chant words I couldn't understand. In others I flew through the sky, or ventured off on underwater expeditions. Miriam often received guidance for her social work, and Ariadne for her artistic endeavors. Saul's dreams continued to be imaginative, beautiful, and compellingly strange—sometimes sexy and at other times filled with bizarre, otherworldly creatures.

One night Sibyl arrived unusually early. She swished through the front door and tossed her patchwork bag near the altar. "You don't mind that I'm early, do you?" She wrapped her arms around me and hummed. "Luce, what have the winds of March blown into your impish presence? Mmm-mmm. I see a dark cloud muddying your aura."

"I wish I knew." I lit candles around the room. She was right, as she often was. Over the previous few weeks I had been feeling depressed for no apparent reason, depleted of energy, and despondent—a condition that seemed to worsen during Sam's trips out of town. Even my dreams were gray and senseless.

Like a traveling magician, Sibyl sat in front of my altar, reached into her bottomless bag, pulled out a miniature deck of Tarot cards, and shuffled. She motioned for me to sit. "I'll do a reading for you." She spread the cards into a circle of twelve, one for each house of the zodiac. Her words stabbed, out of character with her usual jovial presentation.

"Luce, no wonder! Your first house shows cracks splitting open, your world turning inside out with fire and flood, transformation beyond any you've known. The House of Possessions says you might lose something dear. Partnerships will undergo a strain. The House of Secrets shows that someone is undermining you on an unconscious level. Oh, poor Luce. Mmm-mmm. You're strong; you'll get through it okay. Your ninth and twelfth houses show a woman in white guiding you, and you gaining strength through time by yourself."

The door cracked open and Saul poked his head in. I looked at my watch. "Oh, we have to stop! Come on in, Saul."

He sauntered in and crouched over the cards. "She did a reading for you, did she?"

My stomach turned, and I quickly folded the cards into a stack.

He edged in close and sniggered. His fingers, a sea anemone's tentacles, clung to my forearm, producing a surprisingly pleasant sensation.

Sam and I sat in a booth at the Good Earth sipping wine before dinner. "Luce," he said slowly, picking at his nails, then reaching across the table to touch my hand.

I fiddled with my silverware. "Uh-oh. I hate it when you start out like that."

"They're sending me away for six months to train others to do the wilderness program."

The words shattered in my mind like glass. I jerked my hand away. "When?"

"In May." He probed for my hands. I folded them tightly into my armpits.

"Why can't they come *here?*" I held back choked tears, gazed at my wine glass.

He cupped one hand into the other and bumped them to his chin. "The Bay Area is more accessible." His knuckles turned white. "Luce," he said, "I'm coming back."

I couldn't look into his eyes, the clear blue lakes that had always held me to him. I wanted to run, to hide from the gnawing pain that gripped my throat and chest. Feeling abandoned and afraid of falling to pieces in his absence, I had to gather every grain of will not to throw something and stomp out. I slid down in my seat. *I've got to tell him how I feel.* My voice quaked. "Sam," I began, "I've never felt as whole as I have since we began spending time together." My head throbbed. I still couldn't look at him. *I've got to go on.* "Sam, you must know how much I care even though I don't say it . . . I'm not having as many nightmares . . . So much love, so much tender strength." I hid my face in my hands and let tears break an edge that had been guarded for eons.

He rubbed my foot with his. I took a deep breath and wiped my eyes. He leaned across the table and cupped my face in his hands. "I'm coming back, Luce."

That night while I tried to meditate, my mind raced. It sped to the Good Earth Restaurant and Sam, to the splendor of the ocean and the mixed feelings I'd had in my childhood home, to adventures in the mountains and around our cabin, secrets enshrouding my family, frustrations in grade school, failed relationships, and back to Sam. Feelings of confusion and inadequacy tore at me, barring me from every effort to envision the Mother.

I moved to the backyard and bundled into my sleeping bag on the chaise lounge. My eyes settled first on Orion, as they always did. When I was child lying on the roof of our mountain cabin and watching stars glide across the August sky like distant fireworks, Orion was always there. Then with the passing years this constellation, like a lover in a crowded room, continued to show up most clearly—even more so than the Big Dipper, which I invariably had to search for. Orion offered comfort; it was a friend I could count on.

Now gazing into the velvety blackness of space, I could feel the peace of the Mother in the moon, in the arc of constellations, in the universe and the infinite number of universes beyond. *This peace must have something to do with the immortal nectar.* I'd felt it with the Mother and with Sam, both of whom tended to go away like the night sky. *Surely, the immortal nectar, by virtue of its name alone, cannot be something that comes and goes.* I even wondered if Saul and Sibyl were part of my quest for the immortal nectar.

Sam and I met at Saguaro National Monument to ride bikes.

Delilah and Shaman loped along behind. I remained silent for most of the ride, enjoying the whistle of cactus wrens reminding me to remain in the present, not to worry about my past confusions and failures, or about the likelihood of missing Sam in the future. Elf owls poking their heads out of holes in the saguaros offered similar prompts. At the end of the loop, we stretched out under a mesquite tree, Delilah and Shaman resting their heads on Sam's belly.

"I feel a little like you sometimes do," I said. "I just need to be with you and not talk about anything,"

Sam groped for my hand. "Okay."

I contemplated the rows of tiny frondlike leaves overhead, wondered how they knew not to bud until after the last frost of spring. "Just one thing," I said.

"Yeah?"

I turned onto my side, resting my head in my hand, gazing hazy-eyed at the distant olive greens of the palo verdes, creosote bushes, and prickly pears. "Sometimes I think about what you're going to be doing with those prisoners. I'm really glad about it. When I think only of that, and not about your leaving me, I feel happy."

"Thanks." Sam squeezed my hand, slowly rolled his head over, and looked softly into my eyes. "Hey, you know what?"

"What?"

"I really like how you look with your hair growing long—like a forest nymph or something."

Sibyl lingered after the dream group. She slipped her tiny hand into mine, pressed and pumped it almost absentmindedly. "I want to ask a really big favor, Luce. Antonio is having his annual jaguar ceremony next weekend. Women can't be anywhere in sight. The men are afraid of us!" She cackled and then stuttered her humming sound. "Can I stay with you for a couple of days?"

Before I had a chance to respond, she went on. "Don't worry, I'll be unobtrusive, even invisible when your clients are here." She winked. "I'm almost as good as Antonio at shape-shifting."

I flushed, ignorant of the details concerning their powers, and looked away. What was she trying to tell me? She had spoken many times about animal totems, but I'd never fully understood. "Shape-shifting? I thought that stuff referred to just metaphors or archetypes."

Sibyl's giggle turned into a high-pitched squeal. "Luce, you're so funny. Antonio can slip into anything. You never know when he's going to pay you a visit. He especially likes to take on the forms of rattlesnakes . . . and mice."

"Why mice?"

She bounced and shrieked. "Because they get into small places!"

My stomach churned at the thought of his appearing, uninvited, in my house; my neck prickled; and my mind conjured up all sorts of reasons for Sibyl not to stay. Even so, I once again gave in to her request, drawn uncontrollably into her world of magic. *Is it time for my initiatory journey into the underworld she has often alluded to?* I imagined myself entering a damp cave, slipping past gnarly beasts, groping my way through labyrinths, swimming through slime, and finally encountering the object of my quest. "Sure," I said, looking into her eyes, "my house is always open to you, Sibyl."

That night I dreamed of mice crawling through my cabinets, gnawing at the doors, racing around my temple room. I must have let out a sound in my sleep, because Delilah shoved her nose into my face and banged her tail against my bed, waking me up. Images of rodents of all sizes and shapes infested my mind every time I closed my eyes. Even with them open I saw creatures in moist holes in the ground beckoning me to enter.

I switched on the light, rolled out of bed, and stumbled down the hall. *If this is an initiation, it's too scary for me. Didn't Sibyl say I would have a guide through the underworld?* The dogs followed me into the temple room. "Ahh!" I yelled at what I thought was a mouse scurrying across the altar. *My God, I'm imagining things.* Shaman pointed his nose to the ceiling and howled, wagging his tail. I had to laugh. "That's right, Shaman. Scare those mice away."

At an ice cream parlor on Fourth Avenue I sucked on a spoon-ful of hot fudge sundae. "I think my curiosity about feet of toad and eye of newt has turned on me."

"God, Luce, say it in plain English," Sam urged, slurping a root beer.

I rested my chin on my knuckles, still clasping the spoon. "I think I'm in trouble. Miriam, Ariadne, and Coral came over today to tell me what they think is really going on in these dream classes. A couple of months ago they went out to Sibyl and Antonio's place for an all-night ceremony. There they took some hallucinogenic toad juice and danced with Antonio, who later slipped them each a small gift—a crystal, stone, and tiny bundle of sage. Although they'd giggled about it in group, I noticed they were a bit enchanted and didn't want to acknowledge it as a problem. Now they think we're in danger. Miriam says her house is infested with wolf spiders and black widows; Ariadne, swept over with anger, is suddenly having fights with her boyfriend; and Coral has been waking up to knocking sounds on her walls. They're all scared. They think it's because of Antonio, that he's cast some sort of spell by getting them to take home the gifts. And they suspect Sibyl is controlling them psychi-cally through dreams. They've asked me to do something about all this before it goes any further."

Sam popped a maraschino cherry into his mouth. "Do you really expect me to believe you and your friends are being hexed?"

I leaned back in my chair and gazed out the window at the people meandering by. "Sam, I know this sounds weird, but would you call me up a couple of times during the jaguar dance this weekend, just to see how I'm doing?"

He stopped chewing. "You're serious, aren't you?"

Sibyl arrived Friday afternoon. Over dinner she giggled, bab-bling on about Antonio's preparations for the ceremony. "He gets so serious before these things. I think he's mad at me for being jolly before I left."

I tried to smile, joined in by saying, "Oh, how funny." I kept getting up to bring bread, then butter, then tea. *Surely she notices how tense I am.*

"So how have your dreams been, Luce? Did anything come to you about Antonio's gathering?"

Uh-oh, here it comes. "I had some bad dreams about mice . . ."

Sibyl squealed. "Silly girl! Don't let Antonio come into your dreams."

I answered wryly, "I won't let it happen again." Then I looked at my watch. "Time for me to get ready for my therapy group."

Giggling, Sibyl cleared the table. "I'll be quiet while your clients are here, Luce. Really."

Sibyl stayed in the guest room during my group, and afterward I went straight to bed, where I lay shivering, worrying that she was plotting to lead me through the underworld again. This time, I distinctly did not want to go, for fear that once begun such a journey may be irreversible. My muscles tensed. I tried to remain awake, thinking that open-eyed, I would have a better chance of resisting the ordeal. The next thing I knew, however, sunlight was splashing on my face and I had awakened unscathed. *Maybe I'm just being paranoid.*

Sibyl spent most of Saturday visiting friends. When Sam called that afternoon, I had little to report. "I wish we could do something tonight, but I don't feel safe leaving the house with Sibyl here."

"I'm just glad you're okay," said Sam.

Late Sunday morning Sibyl wandered out of her room for tea. Between sips, she confided that she and Antonio had been squabbling recently, although she was reluctant to provide details.

"Luce, would you read the cards for me?" she whined.

My body felt cold. *She's up to something.* I went to make more tea and some toast. "How do you expect me to do that?"

"Oh, Luce. Don't you know by now to just look at the pictures and use your imagination?" She explained the relationship spread and told me to shuffle the cards before beginning.

I took a deep breath, aware that I couldn't say no to her. Despite my trepidation, I was again filled with an uneasy pleasure over the fact that she considered me worthy enough to learn her secrets. I poured tea and nibbled on toast while contemplating the cards.

"Here it looks like Antonio is draping you with a black shawl, doesn't want you to see the flowers falling from the sky or the river in the distance."

"He's keeping things from me, isn't he? Please, Luce, tell me what to do." Her voice was more high-pitched than usual, like a mewling child's.

Having never before seen her in such a helpless state, I felt almost motherly toward her. "Well, the next card is a bit brighter . . ." A sizzling sound distracted me from the reading. Then Delilah barked ferociously, and I jumped up. "What's that noise? Sounds like a broken electric wire."

"No! Don't go out there!" Sibyl screeched.

I threw open the sliding glass door.

Sibyl staggered to her feet, squeezed past me, and planted herself a few yards from the head of a fat rattlesnake that lay coiled in the sand next to the porch, its tail quivering.

"Delilah, come here!" I shouted, slapping my hand against my leg. Delilah looked at me, then back at Sibyl and the snake. "Come here!" She lowered her head and crept over. I grabbed her collar. "Where's Shaman, girl?"

Sibyl was holding her hands in the air, waving her fingers and mumbling to the snake, whom she called Grandfather. Finally, it uncoiled and slithered away.

While facing the snake, she had looked like a priestess of great power. Now, however, her face drooped like that of a chastised twelve year old. "He didn't like it."

"Who didn't like what?" I ran around the yard, searching behind bushes. "Shaman's gone! We've got to find him."

"Antonio. He didn't want you to read for me." She slumped.

"What?" I scurried toward the gate, which was standing open, even though I was sure I had shut it after my morning walk with the dogs.

Sibyl started weeping. "Oh God, please don't let him hurt Luce's dog!"

"What are you talking about?" I darted around the creosote bushes behind the fence. "Shaman?"

Sibyl whimpered as she stumbled along behind me. "I'll help you find him. He's okay. I know he is."

"Who left this gate open?" I tore around the side of the house. "Delilah, go find Shaman! Come on, girl." Delilah sauntered over to smell the garbage pail. "Delilah!"

We searched up and down the road and through the wash, to no avail. Then Sibyl squealed as we rounded the corner back to the cul-de-sac in front of the house. "There he is! You silly old husky, you had us all worried."

Shaman trotted out from the front entryway, panting. He stood still, looking at us, wagging his tail. I dashed to him, wrapped my arms around his neck. "Good boy, you came home." Then I ran my hands through his fur, feeling for snakebite wounds. "He's fine. Thank God."

Sam called Sunday evening after Sibyl had left. "So, is everything okay?"

"Oh, God, you won't believe it." I told him the rattlesnake story while pacing in front of the open sliding glass door.

"That's definitely weird, Luce. What are you going to do?"

I flopped onto the couch and threw my feet up the back of it. "I'm glad you're not leaving for a couple of weeks. I'm afraid something's going to blow." I wound my fingers around the phone cord. "Coral, Ariadne, and Miriam have called most of the members of the dream group. They plan to confront Sibyl."

"Oh, they're going to try to head off a sorceress? Even I know that's not a good idea. Somebody'll fall off a ladder, or get unexplainable sores all over their face," said Sam.

I swung my legs around and looked out the window at Mount Lemmon. "Come on, Sam, this is serious."

"I am being serious," he replied.

After placing a desert daisy on the altar, I lay on my back, with only the candle and a nearly full moon shedding light. My mind whirled. After a failed meditation attempt, singing was the only way to find a little peace: "Oh, holy Mother, comfort me. Let me hear you once more whisper my name. Lonely and frightened, like dust in the wind, I'm lost in this infinite world." As my mind cleared, I recalled the story of the saint who, distracted by the beautiful woman at the river, had forgotten to fetch a glass of water for God. *Why, the same thing has happened to me!*

Confronted with the stark reality of my predicament, I saw clearly that I was stuck in Sibyl's sideshow and had no easy exit. My decision to befriend her had undoubtedly distracted me from searching for the immortal nectar. *Why didn't I listen to the warning bells inside of me?* Oddly, I had found it simpler to trust a whippoorwill's call than my own inner feelings. But then, people often confounded me. Now, I could not imagine how I'd seen any similarity between Sibyl and the Mother.

That night my dreams haunted me. A man with black hair and a mountain lion were stalking me. I sprinted down a lonely shoreline and, with rubber legs, tried to scramble up a cliff. The lion flew through the air at my face. "Hhhaaa!" My own voice woke me up. I was pinned down in my bed, paralyzed. *Antonio! The jaguar ceremony!*

I could hardly drag myself to supervision to tell Pat and Diana about the rattlesnake and Antonio's ceremony. I felt as though the blood had been sucked from my veins. Diana leaned forward, and gazed at me earnestly. "Can you find out what those guys did at the ceremony?"

"Hmm, I bet Ben, the lovely blond fellow from group, would tell me." I felt a sense of hope for the first time, and edged forward in my chair.

Diana glanced at Pat and continued. "I have a friend who's a medicine woman. Her name is Mary. She's part Sioux, seventy years old, a stormwalker, totally on the up and up. Maybe she could offer advice."

In the morning Coral, Ariadne, and Miriam came to discuss our plan. At the dining room table I explained what I'd found out. "Ben let me in on the secrets. The guys learned techniques for using power animals to seduce women and invade dreams. I called Mary, the medicine woman. She said our dream groups must not meet again—ever. That means we mustn't confront Sibyl as a group. Mary said if we aren't together, Antonio and Sibyl can't come after us easily. She also said we must get rid of all leafy plants, as well as anything else they've given us as gifts."

Coral's pixie bangs bounced over her eyes as she slapped her hand on the table and lifted her tea cup in a toast. "Let's do it! Luce, don't forget that philodendron plant Sibyl gave you a few weeks ago."

Ariadne squinted, scrutinizing me. "I hope you'll be okay, Luce."

Sibyl phoned the next day. "Luce, I heard you canceled the dream groups. You have no right. They're my dreamers. I demand their phone numbers!" Sibyl's voice was firm but shrill.

I wrapped myself around and around in the phone cord. "I can't give them to you, Sibyl. People didn't like certain things . . ."

"How dare you! I'm the empress of dreaming. There will be consequences." With that she hung up.

I took a deep breath, slowly set the receiver in its cradle, and untangled myself from the cord. Looking out at the mountain for a long moment, I wondered what to do next. "Come on, Shaman, Delilah! Let's go for a walk." I grabbed the leashes and put my jacket on, then clipped the hook onto Shaman's collar as I always did, simply to get him across the road before letting him run free. But he tugged and pulled as we headed out from the cul-de-sac, causing me to stumble. "Stop it, Shaman!" I jerked on the leash. "Heel!" He turned to at me, tongue hanging out the side of his mouth. "Okay, I know I haven't walked you much these past few days. Go ahead, run."

I unhooked the leash and Shaman bolted ahead. A car sped by, reminding me of the oncoming rush-hour traffic. Dashing down the road, I yelled, "Watch out! Shaman, wait!" He stopped before reaching the intersection and looked at me again, then galloped ahead. Tires squealed. A loud thump. A high-pitched yelp.

"He's dead." My voice was choked. "Shaman's dead," I said to Sam on the phone.

"I'll be right there," Sam replied.

I was hovering over Shaman's body at the edge of the road, with Delilah at my side, when Sam pulled up. He kneeled and touched me gently on the back as I laid my cheek on Shaman's reddish fur and wept. The sun was settling over the Tucson Mountains. After a while my tears subsided and a gradual feeling of expansion filled my heart and stomach. My head felt strangely light. I looked up. "Will you help me bury him?"

Sam straightened up, nodding his head. "Sure."

"I'll go get some things." I raced to the house, gathered a few items into my pack, balanced a shovel over my shoulder, and marched back. Sam carried Shaman to the spot under the desert willow where I had first noticed the husky's otherworldly stare and where the Mother had last appeared. I picked branches from a creosote bush and fronds from a mesquite while Sam dug a hole near the wash. We gently laid Shaman on his blanket, at which point I arranged his legs in a running position. Then I stood up, gazing at his fur glimmering in the moonlight, his closed eyes, his white mask. Circling the grave, I waved a stick of incense and tossed small branches on top of him. "Now you can run, boy. Now you can run all you want." I circled round and round, calling out, "Run, Shaman, run!" Kneeling, I touched him for the last time, passing my fingers across his chest, and covered him with the ends of the blanket. "You're all healed now, aren't you, boy?" I picked up the shovel and briskly pitched sand over him.

Delilah rested her head on the foot of the mound, looking up through her bangs, rolling her eyes to show the whites. I rubbed her ears and, taking Sam's hand, sat beside her. "He was my spirit dog and Delilah's my clown."

"Umm." Sam squeezed my hand.

With my head on his shoulder, I whispered, "The moon will be coming over the Catalinas in a bit. I want to stay here by myself for a while. Would you mind?"

Sam scraped up a handful of sand and let it run through his fingers. "Do you want me to take Delilah back?"

"No, let her stay." I combed my fingers through the mop of hair on her forehead.

"You'll be okay?" asked Sam, standing.

A lump caught in my throat. I looked up at him, fiddled with one of the creosote twigs, and nodded. "I don't know how I could have done this without you."

Sam enveloped me in his arms, kissed me on the forehead, and started to leave. I grabbed his hand, held it to my chest, tears rolling down my cheeks. "Oh, Sam, I loved that dog so much—more than you can imagine."

Sam pressed my hand to his lips. "Shaman was really great."

I sat very still, watching Sam disappear down the wash. Soon, the full moon crested over the top of Mount Lemmon, a giant being watching over the desert. Coyotes yipped in the distance. Delilah growled. "Come on, girl. You know better than to bark at them." She looked up at me, then set her nose down on the sand. Clasping my knees, I rocked back and forth, contemplating the moon. Delilah barked again. Then out of the shadows five or six coyotes appeared and began circling around us. A wildness raised the hair on my skin. I slipped my fingers around Delilah's collar to keep her close by. In unison, half hidden in the faint light behind bushes, the coyotes sang their high-pitched song like infants wailing.

The orb of the moon pulsed to the coyotes' tune, breathing in and out, expanding and contracting. I stared in wonder. Then out of the yellow disc, through one of its hazy veils, I saw the Mother floating down, drifting on eagle wings, her garments glowing. I struggled to my knees, hands in prayer position. She glided across the wash on a river of sand, elegant and white, like the swan that once touched its beak to my palms. I fell to her feet and held her legs, grateful to be welcomed into her magical realm, which felt utterly real and safe, normal and natural, not otherworldly. She lifted me, folded her arms around me, pressing my head firmly against her round belly. "My darling daughter."

I clasped my arms around her waist, sobbing. "I thought you were gone forever."

"I am always with you, child." She rubbed her hands gently up and down my back.

My voice was muffled against her robes. "They killed my dog. Couldn't you have done something?"

The Mother lifted my head, cupping it in her hands. "Child, some things mustn't be interfered with. The laws of nature have to take their course."

I pulled away, my eyes stinging with anger. "I thought you could do *anything!*"

Her smile and touch, as she caressed my forehead, soon melted my fury. After I had calmed down, she sat cross-legged in the sand, her face solemn. "All beings create their own future. Even if I stop an event now, it will take place at some time, in some form. Everything happens for the benefit of each soul and according to the universal laws of balance. Just as gravity causes an apple to fall to the earth, so our actions, both good and bad, cause reactions. A soul's destiny can be postponed, but not prevented. With divine grace, however, the effects of one's negative actions can be minimized. Because of your faith, you lost only your dog."

I pulled my knees up to my chest. "You mean something worse might have happened?"

"Yes, child."

My mind struggled to grasp the meaning of her words. "So Shaman was . . . a sacrifice?"

"Daughter, the dog loved you very much and came into this birth to do a service for you. Similarly, you took pity on him and rescued him from the pet store to give *him* love and affection. He willingly became the target of people who intended to do you great harm."

"My God!" Once more I burst into tears.

The Mother whispered, "Shi, shi, shi," and stroked my chest.

Wiping the wetness from my cheeks, I recalled the events leading up to Shaman's death. "But . . . Mother, why do people commit evil acts?"

"Child, evil is a natural part of creation. People perform bad actions when their desires have become so strong that they lose control of themselves. A spark from a fire meant for cooking may escape into the grass, where a smoldering ember can grow into an unmanageable forest fire. So it is with desire. While our wants are necessary for life, they can easily get out of our control and cause destruction if we are not alert and discriminating. People who are blinded by cravings cannot see their way."

Pondering her words, I gazed at the moon, at the shadows it cast into the mystery of nighttime. "Do these people become lost forever?"

"No, no, child. No one is lost forever. Evil actions can, however, lead to unbearable pain and suffering." The Mother closed her eyes and, rocking, sang in a language I could not understand. Interrupting her song, she held her arms up to the moon and cried out, "Ma, ma, ma, ma." Then she resumed her lullaby, inviting me to rest my head in her lap. The sound of her mellow, raspy voice faded in and out of my consciousness like fragments of a dream.

The cold fingers of night brushed across my cheeks, waking me where I lay curled up beside Shaman's grave, with Delilah as a pillow. I lifted my head to look around. The air was still, not even a whiff of a breeze, and the moon shone high overhead, lighting us with its own kind of warmth. I shivered and struggled to my feet. To arouse my shaggy dog from her slumber, I tapped my pant leg. "Delilah. Come on, girl. Let's go home."

Chapter Six

Sidetracked
by the Macabre

On my morning walk I shuffled along feeling less uplifted than I usually did after a visit from the Mother. Even Delilah lacked her customary bounce. *Had I not been so magnetized to Sibyl and Antonio, Shaman would now be alive.* It was difficult to accept what the Mother had said, that good and evil are facts of creation, that my husky had taken the evil intended for me. I mulled over my encounters with Sibyl, the degree to which I had lost myself in her charm and her magic. How did I get so pulled in?

A family of quails scurried across my path, the little ones racing in single file, never seeming to question where the mother bird was leading them, or whether or not to follow. *I'm just like those little ones running after their mother.* Although I knew now that Sibyl and the Mother were not at all alike, I saw my attraction to them as one and the same. In both instances I was seeking to enter into the unknown and unveil the mysteries of life. As it turned out, the Mother was the true holder of these mysteries whereas Sibyl was merely a carnival fortune-teller, a fascinating sleight of hand. With the Mother, unlike with Sibyl, I'd never felt a sense of danger or a fear that my mind was not my own; I'd felt only love. An enormous ocean of love.

Even so, some of the Mother's messages seemed to contradict one another, which I found confusing. For example, there was "Don't worry about physical and mental well-being" and "Take precautions to sustain that well-being"; "Destiny can't be changed" and the Mother's admission that she could alter fate; "Good and evil are both involved in creation" and "Avoid evil." How was I to figure these paradoxes into my quest for the immortal nectar, which I now supposed had something to do with the soul's constancy and true happiness? Perhaps my task was to strike a balance between the apparent inconsistencies in these teachings. Of one thing I was certain: I wanted only love, forever present, never changing.

The evening after Shaman died, Sam came for dinner. After eating, we sat in the family room lit only by a few votive candles on the coffee table and two half-burned dinner candles. With my voice choked and unsteady, I told Sam what I'd been pondering for hours: "When I was five, I saw my grandfather dead. There was nothing to look at except an empty body. As a child, that made perfect sense. But Shaman's death has been different. At first, I could see that he wasn't in his dead body. Then, I didn't want him to be gone—he was my wolf, my independent spirit. He was such a rascal, always running off, yet I couldn't stand to hold him back or chain him down. Now, I feel a terrible ache inside, a dying in my heart. But maybe now he's really free. Is that how death works? Does it set spirits free?"

Sam sat with his head bent, hands folded in his lap. "I don't know, Luce." Then wiping the tears from my cheeks, he added, "I guess it's whatever we believe it is."

After that, Sam came by every day for lunch or dinner or a walk in the desert. During his third visit, he asked, "How's Delilah doing with Shaman gone? Do you think she still misses him?"

"Do you know what she did this morning?" I replied. "Hours after Shaman died, I put his tennis ball on the altar. Delilah never plays with tennis balls, but after breakfast the next morning she stepped up to the alter almost on tiptoes, clamped her jaws softly around the ball, and took it down. She never touched that ball again. I guess she figured we'd been grieving long enough."

The next day, Sam and I went for a drive. I couldn't imagine where he was taking me, and he wouldn't drop any hints. He said only, "Since I'm leaving next week, I've planned a little outing for us. It's a surprise." We wound along Skyline Boulevard and turned onto a side street that led to the Hacienda del Sol Guest Ranch. Sam didn't usually take to elegant dining, not without a little prodding. In the parking lot he turned off the ignition and looked at me with a slight smirk on his face.

"Sam, you remembered this is one of my favorite spots. But it's only five o'clock. Are they already serving?" We got out and stood arm and arm, staring at the valley below.

Sam swung his hips playfully against mine. "Do you give up?"

"You mean this isn't the surprise?" I grabbed him around the waist and pushed him.

He dashed out of my reach, jumped in the car, and started the engine. "You'll never guess. It's gonna be fun, Luce. You'll see."

We meandered down River Road, passed Swan, and took a right on Craycroft. "Sam, where are we going?"

He just looked at me and grinned.

Off of Grant he pulled into a miniature golf playground that looked like a cross between a papier-mâché Taj Majal and something out of a Walt Disney feature cartoon. Castles, giant men, and huge, colorful monkeys and bears towered against the business district's low-lying buildings.

"You've got to be kidding. This is the surprise?" I doubled over, laughing.

Sam jumped out of the car, ran around to my door, opened it, and tugged on my arm. "It's not as dumb as you think, Luce. See that mouth opening and closing? You've gotta time your swing just right."

From hole to hole we giggled like children, arguing about how many strokes the other had taken, urging moving obstacles to let the ball through, and fighting over who would be first on the next round. Between holes we huddled together on benches, crunched Cracker Jacks, and watched others trying to outguess the course. On our way to the car after the third game, I wound my arm around Sam's. "I'm going to miss you."

His eyes, clear as the Caribbean Sea, penetrated mine. "I'll miss you, too."

I rubbed my shoulder against his arm. "Sam, let's not go out to dinner. Let's buy food and barbecue it on the back porch."

A full moon was rising over the Catalinas when dinner was ready. I had spread a tablecloth and blanket on the sand. A wine bottle and large wooden plate of chicken mixed with skewered corn on the cob were set against a backdrop of creosote bushes and orange ocotillo blossoms glowing like ceremonial torches.

We clinked wine goblets. Sam put his glass to my lips and I dipped into it with my tongue, sipping. He picked up a chicken leg, held that to my lips. When I tried to bite into it, he chuckled, pulled it away, then brought it slowly back. Holding his gaze, I partook of his offering, as if it were an ancient communion dipped in wine and singed in sacred fire. I rubbed a chicken breast across his chin and lips. He grabbed it in his teeth, edged toward me, and still holding it in his lips, pressed it against my mouth. We gnawed, then let the still-fleshy bones fall, our lips touching, softly sliding. His body pressed into mine, undulating like swells on a summer sea.

Our lovemaking was beyond anything I had ever imagined. The earth swirled beneath us, spinning from the ocean floor, bursting through the surface, splashing into the pulsing stars. The dew from the moon moistened our skin as my body drank his juice, sending a gentle surge upward from my heart into his. Afterward, we lay motionless for a long time, our entwined bodies glowing in the midnight moon.

On my porch Monday morning, hours before Sam's departure, we munched on waffles smeared with strawberries and maple syrup. He dropped a piece into Delilah's mouth, then looked at me with ocean-blue eyes. "If I get lonely for you, I'll think back on these last two days, for they'll be imprinted on my mind forever. I'll remember you even during the wildest storm in the deepest mountain wilderness."

I lowered my head. Right away, I could feel myself about to change the subject and make snippy comments to avoid revealing anything too intimate. Instead, I said: "Sam, my feelings for you are deep and clear, like an alpine stream. Maybe you're the immortal nectar I'm to discover. Yet I'm nervous about what will happen after you leave and whether these emotions of mine will ever be constant."

He pulled his chair around and took both my hands. "Luce, remember how we lay on the bed in the candlelight last night, just looking into each other's eyes for what seemed like an eternity? Those feelings can't go away—not ever. While we're apart from each other, let's do this: when we close our eyes to go to sleep, let's feel that we're soaring up to the stars together, or climbing hills covered with flowers, or splashing in mountain streams."

I nudged my forehead against his and took a deep breath. "Okay."

A week passed and I didn't hear from Sam. He had told me he wouldn't always be near a phone, but I'd never imagined his absence would be this hard. I crumpled onto a pile of pillows in front of my altar. *Mother, please make Sam call. I so badly want the nearness of his love. Or am I supposed to be as detached from him as I am from the Catalina Mountains, or the night sky?*

The yellow eyes of the coyote on the poster drilled into me, melting my churning mind. Once again I attempted to meditate and ended up singing instead: "Let my spirit fly to you—no place could be too far. Remove this cloud of ignorance, and show me where you are."

What am I going to do for six months without Sam? My mind drifted back to the summer when my dad sometimes visited. I was five, and we'd go to Whispering Sands Beach for picnics, strolling down the silty dirt trail between the ice plants covering the knoll. No other beaches in our small town had sand that squeaked like a burst of wind through pines when my heels dug into it. I'd skip over the waves and bend down, stretching my hands to catch the tinkling gush of water washing through broken shells and sand. My dad would carry me into the deep, channel-like tide pools whose mouths emptied directly into the sea. He taught me to paddle and kick, and to float on my back, bobbing along on the ocean swells like a baby duck.

Now I wondered about escaping to an ocean. *Maybe to Hawaii's Big Island and those caves I've heard about.* I was startled out of my daydream by a knock at the door. *That's strange. I don't have clients today.* I peered through the glass peek-a-boo bubble. *Saul!* My heart skipped a beat. Dizzy, I steadied myself against the wall. He knocked again, harder. I opened the door, stepped outside. "Hi, Saul. How come you didn't call first?" Delilah pushed though, banging her tail against the door, and sniffed at Saul's pant legs.

"I wanted to talk to you in person. I . . . didn't know if you'd agree to see me— you know, after all that happened with Sibyl and Antonio." His face was solemn and his eyes steady.

I tapped the door closed and let Delilah wander outside. "That's definitely a consideration."

"They've left town, you know," said Saul.

"No, I didn't know." I leaned my shoulder against the adobe wall, my arms folded.

He drummed his fingers on his knuckles. "Their house burned down."

I cast my eyes toward the ground; my stomach churned. *Good!*

His voice emerged through a thick fog. "You know, I really didn't approve of some of their practices."

Looking into his eyes, I asked, "How did you come to that?"

"The stuff they were teaching started to affect my music." Saul held his hands as if he were playing the organ, then curled his fingers and stiffened them. "I got frozen inside. The passion was gone."

I pushed the doormat around with my foot.

One side of his mouth turned up in a sort of half smile as he edged closer to me. "Can we have dinner sometime?"

"I have a boyfriend. I thought everyone knew that," I said.

"Does that mean you can't you have male friends?" He managed a grin that revealed dimples.

I slapped my leg to call Delilah and held her collar. "I told you in dream class that time must pass before I have friendships with former clients."

"That's why I quit the therapy group. I figured you weren't supposed to fraternize with clients. Almost a year has passed since then." He touched the tips of his fingers together, stretching them back. "I was hoping to be your friend."

My heart thumped; my fingers felt cold and moist. I opened the door, shoved Delilah into the house. "Why don't you give me a call. I'll need a little time to think about it."

"Okay," he said, ducking his head and slinking down the driveway.

That evening Sam called.

"You've no idea how glad I am to hear your voice. Just this morning I pleaded with the Mother to have you call."

He chuckled. "Magic, huh?"

I pulled the cord over to a dining room chair and sat down. *Should I tell him about Saul?* "How's the training going?"

"I've got a bunch of guys, social workers, I'm taking into the wilderness for two weeks. Then we'll come back and do didactic stuff before taking the prisoners out."

"Are you excited?" I got up and wandered around the room as far as the cord would let me. As happy as I was to be talking to Sam, I couldn't get Saul off my mind.

"A little nervous. I hope I do okay."

I slid open the door between the kitchen and living room, and studied my altar. "I'll ask the Mother to help you!"

"Uh-oh, does that mean I might start seeing things, too?"

I laughed. "I'm also going to ask her to help me feel your love across this agonizing distance."

"Luce, I hold you as I fall asleep at night."

My heart warmed, spreading rivulets of love through my body. "I hold you, too."

Coral took the hot seat in therapy group. She sat with her back straight and toes pointed, as if rehearsing a ballet pose. "My sister, nine years older than me, used to go out the second-story bedroom window and down a pine tree—to escape without our mom knowing. I wanted to go, too. So one day I scurried downstairs, asked my mom for my little red chair, dragged it to the bedroom window and climbed out. I leaned over, but was too short to reach the tree. The rest is blank. Except I remember when the doctor came. My mother was crying, holding me in her rocking chair. She says I kept telling her, 'Don't cry, Mommy.' Obviously, I wasn't hurt too badly."

Coral stiffened, and tightened her mouth. " I was so busy taking care of my mom that I didn't have invisible friends like everybody else here." By the end of the session, Coral had gotten in touch with the terror of falling out the window and realized her mom wasn't her responsibility. She described the session this way: "Something inside me melted. Then all these pictures from my fairy-tale books of long ago started to float through my brain—their characters alive and dancing, singing. I feel totally free."

Lord only knows why I accepted an invitation from Saul to meet at church for a chamber music concert. I told myself it was because I loved music, or maybe because I felt sorry for him. But a stickiness in my stomach, a lingering ache, forced me to admit that he was not merely a source of good entertainment to me, or someone to rescue. Why was I so attracted to him? Was it the magic again, the lure of the occult? No, it was more than that. It was a fascination with the underworld of slimy creatures, their masked, muddy mouths open and hollow, and their slippery bodies surrounded by scores of translucent insects, crawling, writhing, coupling, chewing. *My God! Never before have I felt such an obvious pull toward the macabre.*

The concert included a short Buxtehude organ solo performed by Saul. At the end he sauntered over to me with a dimpled grin. "So, what'd you think?"

The first time I'd noticed his dimples was outside my front door when he had shown up unannounced. *He's sort of attractive.* "I didn't know an organ could sound like that mellow—like oboes and bassoons."

"This organ is mechanical, not electric. The ones in most American churches are electric. And many musicians don't know how to use the subtleties of a good organ. I trained in Europe and then toured, playing in many well-known churches. When it comes to mechanical instruments, you have to know how to press the pads of your fingers down just so." He moved his fingers up and down on the back of his hand. "There can be a little wind sound if you don't hit the keys exactly right."

He's led a very interesting life. "I always shut organ music off when I hear it on the radio." I said. "Now I'll have to pay more attention."

He laughed—not with a snicker, but rather with a genuine chuckle—and his green eyes held a steady gaze. "You said we might have lunch or breakfast sometime. You want to go to La Paloma's Sunday brunch? They lay out quite an elegant feast. It would have to be after church, of course."

What am I going to do? I wandered over to the display of pamphlets and thumbed through them. "Not this week. Maybe next Sunday. If I decide to come, I'll attend the church service and meet you here."

Diana and I strolled along the path above the dry bed of the Rillitto River. Delilah sniffed along behind. Even though it was only nine o'clock in the morning, the air already hot. "I went to a concert at Saul's church. He was actually charming, and delightfully enthusiastic about his music."

Diana's cheeks reddened. "What about Sam, Luce?"

We dipped into the riverbed, our footsteps breaking the muffled silence of the desert air. "Nothing could come between Sam and me. Saul just wants to be my friend. He's a bit of a loner, and I guess I feel sorry for him."

Diana put her hand on my arm and stopped. "Luce, don't you remember how you got sucked in when he was in therapy with you?"

I dug my big toe into the sand. "The Mother said people act in evil ways because they can't control their desires. Saul told me he's *given up* that sorcery stuff. Besides, he's a talented organist."

"What does that have to do with it? Oh, Luce. The Mother said you'd have to go over hurdles. I'd just hate to see this be the next one."

I dreaded the thought of not hearing from Sam now that he was in the wilderness. Morning and evening meditations brought occasional solace, and imagining myself in his arms as I fell asleep satisfied some of my longing for him. However, I had to force my restless mind to be still long enough to do these practices. In the meantime, nightmares of a man pursuing me intensified. The greatest and most humiliating difficulty was controlling my thoughts about Saul. I tried to brush away this now familiar obsession, this bottomless hole deep inside me sucking me in. In the midst of my despair I dreamed that after Sam and I had climbed a mountain, I slipped off the pathway, and as I dangled from the edge of the cliff, he grabbed me. I woke in a sweat.

On a rare night of peace, I dreamed that Sam and I lay beside each other on a log raft, floating down a wide, meandering river. The sun bleached everything white. Our bodies, wrapped around a column of light, spiraled into the sky, where they began soaring like eagles. The image pulsed with so much life that when I awoke I was certain Sam lay next to me. When I felt him rise and drift out of the room, I rolled out of bed after him, following him down the hall and into the bathroom. I reached out to touch him, grasping at air, the shower curtain, then searching high and low, only to realize he wasn't there. After that I was left with a craving I could hardly bear.

At La Paloma Resort's outdoor breakfast buffet in the Catalina foothills, Saul and I sat under the arbor, refreshed by mist from outdoor coolers. We filled our plates with lavish choices—eggs Benedict, bacon, sausage, salmon, capers, berry tarts, mango, papaya, cinnamon rolls, croissants, and more. The exquisite view of saguaros and mountains ought to have been relaxing, but instead I found myself squirming in my seat, unable to reconcile my love for Sam with my willingness to join Saul for breakfast.

Saul skillfully peeled a mango, cut it into slices, and slid them into his mouth. "I don't know if I told you I was a novitiate in a Benedictine monastery."

Choking on my sherry, I sputtered. "I beg your pardon."

"I was a monk in training," he said, now sucking on the mango pit.

I sipped more sherry to stop coughing. "That's what I thought you said."

He cackled, his eyes glimmering. "I wanted to be the principal organist. But what I found was that even in the monastery I could make people do things. Once, while another novitiate was giving a concert, I sat in the balcony and sent laser beams out through my eyes, causing him to flounder over the keys. I felt so bad, I eventually left the monastery. Using spiritual energy to cause accidents to unsuspecting brothers just didn't seem right, if you know what I mean." He paused to take a sip of his Riesling. "But the main reason I didn't take vows was that I was getting really horny."

My mouth hung open; a piece of salmon dropped off my fork and into my lap. *Diana's right—he's creepy. But fascinating. I'm definitely off track.* A craving gnawed like vultures inside my chest as I pried the fish off my dress.

Saul's unruly hair, pointed chin, and dimpled cheeks made him look like the god Pan. He slipped the mango pit out of his mouth and began nibbling on a cherry tart. "At the monastery there was a secretary named Isabel. She was always stopping to talk, sometimes stepping so close that I'd swoon from the lilac perfume on her hair. I could tell she liked me. What woman doesn't want to seduce a monk? One day Isabel and I were alone in the library, and she looked at me with moist eyes, asked if I wanted to go for a walk, said she needed to talk about some problems. So we went out into the woods. There she took my hand, pulled me into the hills where huckleberries grow. She sat me down under a wild oak, unbuttoned her dress, and pressed herself against me. Then she slowly unsnapped my shirt and unzipped my pants. We rolled in the soft grass and fallen oak leaves, losing ourselves in the warmth of passion."

The more he spoke, the more I had to stifle my breath.

He raised his eyebrows. "You like that story, don't you?"

I swallowed hard and stood up to get more food. "I'll be back in a minute."

Delilah pulled me along the neighborhood road past flat-roofed adobe houses. Images of Saul preyed on my mind: his green eyes, pointed chin, huge hands. Our breakfast conversation haunted me. *Why had he wanted to become a monk? Why did that one incident lure him away from his spiritual pursuits? Or didn't it?*

I figured he'd happened upon some unusual way to combine sex and spirituality, yet his mind was so peculiar, perhaps even perverted, I couldn't possibly imagine what it was. And like a fool, I wanted to know. I wondered if Saul's sexual deviations were similar to my dad's, who had apparently endeared himself to many women.

"Delilah, what do you think, girl? Does he want more than a friendship?"

She looked at me and wagged her tail.

During intermission at a symposium on medieval witchcraft, I asked Saul, "What pleasure do you get from making people trip, or spill coffee, or fumble over organ keys? And how is this related to your earlier spiritual path?"

"Oh, I do a lot more interesting things now." He snickered. "I've gone way beyond that amateurish stuff Antonio and Sibyl do. It's not good to misuse powers, and I really don't want to hurt people anymore. The work I now do is meant to be healing."

I sipped on instant coffee. "Is this work connected with your original desire to be a monk?"

His face went slightly pale, and the corners of his mouth turned down.

I looked into his eyes, trying to find clues in their dark green pools. "I don't mean to probe. I just want to know if the two are in any way linked."

He drummed his fingers on the Styrofoam cup. "For me to answer that question we'll have to have dinner together at a really comfortable place."

Unsure if I was willing to go out for another meal with Saul, I changed the subject. *Maybe I can find out about the sex-spirituality connection in some other way. It certainly has a nectarlike lure.*

At last, Sam called. As we talked, I slouched, with my legs propped up on a chair. My nerves were jangled. No longer could I brush Saul off as a mere distraction. I felt like a heretic, but didn't know how to tell Sam about it over the phone. My voice cracked. "Sam, it's hard to go so long without hearing your voice. Delilah misses you, too. Can't you come home for a weekend?"

"Maybe later, Luce. Did you notice something special the other night? After the guys had all gone to sleep, I stayed by the campfire, closed my eyes, and felt you with me more clearly than anything."

My heart warmed, swelled as I twirled the phone cord around my fingers. "Is that really true, Sam?" I told him about my dream, and how I had seen him walking down the hall and into the bathroom.

He was quiet, pulsing inside of me. Then he said, "I've never known anything like this, have you?"

"Never." It was difficult to understand why, during such moments of extreme tenderness, Saul lurked in the corners of my mind.

Steadily, I slipped into the quicksand of Saul's obscure charm. I sensed the same magnetism I'd felt with Sibyl, but convinced myself that this situation was different. After all, I was no longer interested in magic practices and there was nothing occult I was hoping to learn from him. Under the pretense of wanting to hear him practice the organ, I accepted his invitation to go to church. I perched next to him on the bench in the empty sanctuary while he played a Bach sonata. His eyes shone with devotion. He caressed the keys in communion, his fingers like lilies, his music the hymn of the Ascension. He undulated, dripping with sweat, his face writhing in ecstatic agony. My soul reverberated like cello strings, and I fell limp.

We met at the church frequently, sometimes several times a week. As we walked out after practice one day, he took my hand in his. I pretended to regard his warm and steady grip as a friendly gesture, a European expression of affection. After that, every time we left the house of worship he held my hand. My body tingled from the electricity of music still flowing from his fingers.

While leaving the church one Thursday afternoon, Saul took my hand and asked, "When are you going to invite me to your house for dinner?"

I immediately withdrew my hand. "I already told you I have a boyfriend."

Saul planted himself in front of me, his eyes penetrating mine. "Well, where is he?"

I clasped my hands behind my back. Stuttering, I replied, "He's away . . . for a little while."

Saul's body towered over mine and was now within inches of me. "Then maybe we can have dinner once in a while until he comes back."

I was strangely attracted to his aggressive stance and piercing eyes. My heart pounded erratically. I wondered if his fingers touched everything as passionately as they touched the organ keys. My voice was hot and dry. "When do you want to come?"

His pale fingers brushed my neck, slipped down my back, and lingered on my clutched hands. "Saturday night."

In therapy group the next day we continued to work on childhood experiences in nature and with invisible friends. Throughout
the session, the memory of Saul's green eyes kept creeping into my
mind. Ben shook his blond hair out of his face as he told a story
about getting lost while fishing with his dad. "After thrashing
through underbrush for a while, I wrapped my arms around a tree
just like I used to around my grandmother's apron-covered legs.
'Trees know everything,' she used to say. So I looked up at the
branches and asked, 'Mr. Tree, can you help me find my daddy?'
Right away, a little gray chattering squirrel ran down just inches
from me—*tsk-tsk-tsk*. It scooted around my feet until I realized I was
supposed to follow it. I ran after that little critter all the way to the
place along the bank where I had been fishing with my dad. The
squirrel scurried a short distance downstream, stood on its hind legs,
and chattered some more. I followed, and within minutes I found
my dad." Ben's face lit up like a child's. "I bet that squirrel is what's
now running around inside my head and driving me crazy because
I'm not letting it show me what to do."

After the group members left, I went outside to pick a few
mesquite leaves for the Mother before I meditated. Mortified at the
way my thoughts had drifted to Saul during the session, I was eager
to close my eyes and clear my mind. Even as I brought the Mother's
image into my vision, however, memories of Saul's fingers on the
organ keys and of his hand holding mine invaded my inner world.
No amount of concentration could prevent my groin from pulsing
with warmth at the recollection of sitting beside him on the organ
bench. With persistence, however, I soon slipped into an expanded
feeling—that sense of vast space I had often experienced in the
Mother's presence. I heard the words she had said next to Shaman's
grave: "People perform bad actions when their desires have become
so strong that they lose control of themselves."

My eyes popped open. What twisted hunger, what distorted rapture had driven me into this unwanted yearning for Saul? I had to
admit that I was sexually attracted to him and at the same time
repulsed by him. On the other hand, everything about Sam—his gentleness, the constancy of his love, his understanding, and our physical
lovemaking—was in keeping with my search for happiness. The more

I thought about this dilemma, the more I realized my interest in Saul was deranged. First, it had to do with some tormented aspect of my father. *If this is the only way to know my father, I want nothing more to do with it.* And second, it was spurred on by my attraction to the dark side of life, my fascination with evil. *I've lost my dog as a result of this obsession. I refuse to lose anything else, and I hope it's not too late.*

I decided to proceed with the dinner invitation, fearful that canceling it would cause Saul to seek some irreversibly destructive form of revenge. However, I planned to ensure that this dinner would be our final rendezvous. To make the scene as unromantic as possible, I turned on all the lights and set the table inside, where the monsoon season brought a sticky warmth to the air. Stepping out to the porch, I began to prepare dinner, all the while glancing nervously at my watch. *He's late.* Then he knocked. I wiped my hands on my apron, hurried to open the door, greeted him with a "Hi, Saul," and rushed back to the shish kebab.

He sidled up behind me, pressed his body against my back, and grasped my hand, skewer and all. "Let me help you," he offered.

My mind swirled. Wedged me between him and the barbecue, like Prometheus pinned to rock cliffs, my body rippled with fear and pleasure, then sank, off balance, into him. I slipped my hand out of his grasp, wiped the perspiration from my face and neck. *God, why is my body responding to him so readily?* It was Sam who'd awakened me to the pleasures of intimacy—someone I was not about to be unfaithful to.

Saul blew gently on my neck, whispering, "I like the heat. Don't you?"

My body trembled with a primeval fear I'd known only in dreams and in the Chiricahua Mountains. "Actually, I'd like a little wine to cool down. Could you take this skewer for a minute?" I twisted away, leaving him juggling the shish kebabs.

He followed me inside, however, and began opening and closing the kitchen cabinets, finally pulling out a pair of red candles and holding them up triumphantly. "Let's eat on the porch!" he insisted, then he picked up the place settings, moved them outside, turned off the porch lights, and lit the candles.

I kept my eyes on him as I loaded a tray with a bottle of Bordeaux, a bowl of green olives, a basket of crackers, and a wooden board for slicing cheese. I gingerly set the tray on the table, searching my mind for a graceful exit. *I'll run out the gate if he gets too intense. But I'll need my car keys.* "Here, we can munch on these while the meat cooks. But I forgot napkins. I'll be right back." I sauntered inside, trying to appear casual, then slipped the keys into my pocket and returned with linen napkins.

He must have sensed my suspicion, because he pulled back, relaxed into his chair, and launched into a discussion about a lecture he had attended on women who were persecuted during the Spanish Inquisition. His description of the events, trials, and burnings were cool, almost scientific. I shivered, convinced that in a sexual relationship he'd be dangerously perverse.

The Bordeaux calmed me, as did the shish kebab, which was delicious. By the time I served carrot cake for dessert, we had finished the wine and I was thoroughly bewitched from watching Saul's dimples flash and eyebrows arch as he described further outings with the secretary at the monastery. "Our encounters were wild; I'd last for hours without losing my potency. After leaving the monastery, I stayed with her for a couple of years until I went to Europe on a music grant. By the time I got to France, I was a better lover than any Frenchman. My girlfriend there told me she had never had so many unrestrained peaks of delicious pleasure in a single night."

My body rippled into a slowly bubbling volcano of desire. All of a sudden, Saul was standing behind me, his hands gently and firmly grasping my breasts. I swooned and swelled. The next thing I knew, we were on my bed. He was fondling me, unbuttoning his clothes and mine. Then as if from nowhere, Sam's face appeared before my eyes. I bolted upright, shoved Saul off me, dashed out of the room, and headed for the front door.

He tore after me. "Come back here!"

My fingers were on the doorknob when he planted his hand

over mine and blocked the door with his foot. I yelled, "Get away from me—*now!*"

Saul withdrew his hand, but left his foot wedged against the door. He lifted his arms, arching his wrists like a bullfighter preparing to thrust in the banderillas. His eyes had sunk deep into their sockets, and his eyebrows were pointed. Then he slowly lowered his hands and wrapped his fingers, smooth and cold, around my neck. "You loved what I was doing, and you know it," he said.

As Saul pressed his fingers into my flesh, my mind cleared like the lifting of a summer fog. Instinct told me not to say a word but to look calmly and deliberately into his eyes, at Mephistopheles himself, chilly and piercing. We stood locked together like that for a long moment. Then gradually his face softened and he released his grip, slumped over, covered his eyes with his hands.

I acted quickly, sneaking off toward the family room, eyes glued to the sliding glass door. Suddenly, I heard Saul racing through the temple room and into the kitchen, where he picked up the meat knife and, stalking me, blocked my way to the sliding door. I froze. His eyes were wide, the whites shining, and black centers, like beads of fire, circled with phosphorescent green. He crouched and crept forward. I couldn't move. Suddenly, as if gripped by an invisible force, he dropped the knife, clutched his chest, and fell to the ground. Writhing on the tiles, his face contorted in pain, he moaned, "Call a doctor." Then he curled into a fetal position and lay still.

In the sticky silence I edged over to him step-by-step, leaned down, grabbed the knife, and tossed it toward the kitchen. His face was like a small child's, and his hands reached out to me as I bent over him. Tears fell down his cheeks. Hesitating at first, I grasped him under the arms. "Can you get up?"

Saul struggled to his feet, still holding his chest. Filled with unexpected pity for this lost soul, I led him to the couch and gently set him down. I was too terrified to let him stay and, at the same time, wanting to comfort him. *Why am I doing this? I should be calling the police.* I lifted his head, rested it on my lap, and began stroking his face, whispering, "You're going to be all right." His face was clammy and wet, and he soon fell asleep, his fingers still probing like octopus tentacles.

I cradled and rocked him as he slept, supplicating to the Mother to relieve him of his agony. After some time, I got up to make tea and Saul awoke. "Please don't leave me," he pleaded.

Still frightened about what he might do next, I sat back down and rubbed his chest. "Are you feeling better?"

He nodded, reached out to pull me to him, but I slid away. *I've got to get him out of here.* "Do you think you can drive now?" I asked sweetly.

His reddened eyes begged with me to let him stay. With my arm around his neck, I lifted him to a sitting position, whereupon he hung his head, narrow shoulders drooping, fingers drumming on his knees. Then I guided him out the door into the moonless night. He leaned on my arm, shuffling his feet, then hunched over in front of his car. I opened the door and gently shoved him in. *Thank you, Mother, for letting him leave so easily.*

Before shutting the door, I pushed the lock down, then backed up a few steps. "Where's your key?"

He clasped the wheel and sat motionless, eventually stuffing his hand in his pocket and pulling out a key chain. He started the car and slowly drove off.

As he headed down the street, the terror of what I'd just been through struck me with full force. *He nearly killed me!* I dashed into the house, locked the doors, then scurried with Delilah out the back gate and through neighboring yards. I raced to the wash, where I roamed for hours, reviewing my escapes from dream figures, the bushman, Sibyl, and now Saul—the most unknown to the most familiar, the most intangible to the most corporeal. The Mother had said I'd be crossing hurdles, but was I any closer to knowing the immortal nectar, or to living with detachment? I could tell I was at least closer to understanding the value of distancing myself from physical and mental desires. *My God, I'm dense. I hope the shock of this encounter with Saul will keep me striving to know what lies beyond the body and the mind.* Certainly, the caring-and-detachment para-dox felt clear: I could be concerned for the welfare of others while maintaining an air of discernment and dispassion.

When I thought it was too late for Saul to come back, I returned home. Exhausted, I fell asleep without another thought.

In the morning I awoke early. While lying in bed, I struggled to unravel the knots in my mind. I endeavored to make sense of my compulsion to rock Saul in my arms after he'd attempted to kill me; but try as I might, I couldn't grasp the bonds of fate that had attached me to him. Deeply ashamed and frightened, I wondered how I could possibly tell Sam about the evening and whether I'd ever trust myself again. Worse yet, would the Mother return after what I'd done?

Because physical activity usually helped clear my mind, I ventured out with Delilah into the still-cool morning air. After walking through the wash and over hills for more than two hours, however, I found no peace. Then, as if from nowhere, an idea implanted itself in my mind: since I had no clients scheduled for Monday, I would park my car on another street so Saul would think I had gone away, then I'd lock myself inside to meditate, contemplate, and write. In between I would stroll through the desert and rest my body in the warm sand. Inspired by stories I had read about desert ascetics, I would follow their example, purifying mind and body by drinking tea and eating only fruit.

On the way home from hiding my Honda, I spotted Saul's car curving around the cul-de-sac. I dashed behind a creosote bush, holding Delilah's collar for fear she would give us away, and remained out of sight. Saul paused at my driveway, rolled down his window, peered around for a long while, then crept away. About a minute after he pulled back onto the main road, Delilah and I raced toward the front door. At that moment a page from a magazine, seemingly out of nowhere, glided through the air and landed at my feet. It contained a photograph of a mountain lion, causing me to shudder. *The jaguar ceremony again.* Was this a mark of Saul's magic or just some stray piece of paper? The chill in my body told me to suspect the worst.

Inside, I contemplated dialing 911. But what would I say—that some magician was after me with a cougar? Wouldn't such a message only bring more attention my way than I cared for? Surely, I decided, prayer and meditation would be my strongest sources of protection. After a sparse lunch of grapes, banana, and kiwi, I sat in prayer. Then I began to record in my journal the events of the previous two months, hoping to more easily recognize my patterns of going astray.

What I found was that my body seemed to have a warning system of its own: it would tingle or shudder to announce impending danger. For starters, I told myself, that would be a reliable cue to follow.

Come evening, after a couple of hours of meditation, I sat crumpled in front of my altar. Having promised myself to meditate till at least midnight, I forced myself awake by breathing deeply. Every once in a while Saul's image, dim and shadowy, would appear superimposed on Sam's. Other times, I would be strolling through the desert holding hands with both of them, Saul on my left and Sam on my right. Mostly, my mind replayed the agonizing evening with Saul. Still, in spite of the painful mental pictures, which I attributed to echoes of the past, I enjoyed a few moments of quiet, and at midnight staggered to bed.

My alarm went off at five o'clock. I dragged myself to my temple room, lit the candle, and as always, began my meditation session by imaging the Mother. My mind meandered in and out of dreamlike scenarios, from grocery shopping and client sessions to childhood events too muddled and murky to identify. At times I was haunted by muddy lake bottoms where Saul and Sam were intertwined like enormous roots. I wrote down the details while in my temple room, speculating: Why are their images appearing in tandem? Is Saul going to plague me forever? I was desperate to understand more about the terrible ache inside me that had caused me to betray Sam. My attempts to remain detached—to witness my mind's tormented ramblings without getting caught up in them—failed repeatedly. Filled with remorse, I prayed for forgiveness, and thanked the Mother repeatedly for delivering me from my own foolishness, aware that no one but she could have caused Saul to lose resolve and collapse in his moment of power.

At dusk on Monday, I walked with Delilah through the wash and, for the first time, began to feel a trace of joy rising in my heart. Back in my temple room, a sense of the numinous continued as I lit my candle for evening meditation. This time, instead of closing my eyes to visualize the Mother, I kept them open and gazed at the framed whiteness that represented her. Faded hues began to swirl inside the frame, turning to rainbows of color. I shut my eyes tightly, then opened them again, only to see the same phenomenon increase in intensity. After a while, the bands of colored light seemed to come together, forming a green valley with a running stream. I heard birds twittering. I sparkled with joy as a verse from Psalms coursed through my mind, "Yea, though I walk through the valley of the shadow of death, I will fear no evil, for Thou art with me . . ." Then I chanted these words aloud over and over again until the rhythm of the sacred verse mingled with the sound of bubbling laughter. I swung my head around to behold the Mother sitting cross-legged behind me, her face beaming like the midnight sun.

A radiance from thousands of stars shone out from within me. I scrambled to my knees and pressed my forehead to the floor. My fingers, like broken-winged birds, crawled across the rug to her feet. She slipped her petal-like fingers into my hand and lifted me to a sitting position.

I bowed my head.

She stroked it. "Child, you have discovered the power of uncontrolled desire, have you not?"

I nodded, tears trickling down my cheeks.

With her white cloth she wiped my eyes. "Daughter, among millions of people, thousands desire to be free. Yet only a small number of these will come to know the truth of the immortal nectar. The lure of the world, with its many attractions, is so great that even the most sincere fall prey to its enchanting web."

I swam in the clear, deep lakes of her eyes. I longed to discover how she knew everything and who she really was.

As though reading my thoughts, she smiled enigmatically. "I am the love that flows through all things. I am the yellow blossoms of palo verde trees in springtime and Orion in the dark of night. I am the coyotes howling under the moon and the splendor of the Catalina Mountains. I am the torrential rains of summertime and the intoxicating juice of the saguaro fruit. I am all these and more."

The fluid of her black eyes warmed my soul. Soon, however, memories of my errors with Saul interrupted my reverie. "What about my love for Sam?" I asked. "Will it be lost forever because of this?"

She tickled me under the chin and chuckled. "A long time ago there was a god-man who stole the hearts of all the women in a small farming village. One full-moon night, he played his lute to lure them to the river. He knew they wanted to make love to him.

But when they arrived at the edge of the waters, the god-man hid. The women were beside themselves with agony. They raced through the bushes, tearing their clothing and scratching their skin on brambles, crying out, 'My Lord, where are you?' Finally when, through their desperate and earnest search, their minds and hearts had become purified, he stepped out from his hiding place. The women, whose eyes now sparkled like moonlight on the river, formed a circle and danced around him in the emerging light of dawn. Through their longing for the god-man, they had discovered pure love—the essence of all creation. In the same way, your love for Sam can dip you into the immortal nectar and take you to my abode in the snowy mountains of eternal bliss. But your love for him must be unconditional. If it is your earnest wish, I can make your desire for pure love so unflinching that nothing will ever break it. But it is up to you, child."

The Mother closed her eyes, her lips forming the most tantalizing smile I had ever seen. While I stared in wonder at her countenance, there floated above her head images of snow-capped mountains and celestial beings, chariots drawn by swans, and carpets of flowers. High-pitched stringed instruments and flutes harmonized with birds chirping and chortling. The scent of rose infused the air.

It was still dark when I realized my head was slumped on my chest. I rested my eyes on the plain white silk in the picture frame. Although the brilliance of the Mother's love was all that remained, I lingered in that bed of roses for a long time.

Chapter Seven

River of Fire

The Mother's fragrance lingered on whiffs of breezes, and I caught glimpses of her garments drifting behind creosote bushes and palo verde trees. I pulled off my shoes and skipped through the wash, splashing sand with my feet, spreading my arms to fly. Delilah pounced and circled me.

The sun peeked over the Catalinas, quickly warming the air. A few thunderheads gathered in the south, the last vestiges of monsoon season. Momentarily sobered, I explored my dilemma: How could I be certain Saul wouldn't try to invade my life again? My terrifying experience with him made me realize the extent to which I'd failed to take command of my day-to-day existence. While tumbling around from one emotionally charged event to another and continuing to harbor fascination for life's shady side, how could I expect to find the immortal nectar?

I paused at a respectful distance to observe a tarantula ambling along, its hairy legs padding gingerly across the sand. The spider's slow, steady gait contrasted sharply with my own tendency to dart here and there, getting sidetracked each step of the way. *I need to be more focused on my goal, to let the Mother's presence permeate every second of my life.*

To strengthen my resolve, I no doubt required more time alone, unencumbered by phone calls or visitors. Yet if I stayed home, I would constantly worry that Saul might show up unannounced.

A lizard scurried under a rock. *Taking charge of my life is not a matter of how slow or fast I go. It has more to do with being aware of my own nature and acting with integrity.* Suddenly, I knew what to do: I would go out of town on retreat for a couple of weeks. Turning toward home, I quickened my pace. It felt right to leave now, despite my inability to let Sam know, even though the Mother had said he was intimately connected to furthering my quest for the immortal nectar. As I scurried past mesquite trees and chollas, images floated through my consciousness of sandy shores, rocky cliffs, a turquoise sea with dolphins leaping through waves, and caves I'd always wanted to visit. Yes, I decided, I would go to Hawaii.

Back home, I ate breakfast and then phoned Diana. I summarized my encounter with Saul and the key realizations that had surfaced during my two-day retreat.

"My God, Luce. Something even worse might happen. I never could understand your obsession with that man."

I dragged the phone to the porch and sat on the chaise lounge. "Believe it or not, your advice rang out to me—at first from the back of my mind, and then loud and clear. I can't thank you enough. Now I need to get away. My friend Gwendolyn, who lives on the Big Island in Hawaii, works at a resort called Kalani Honua and has made a reservation for me there. My flight leaves the day after tomorrow. I'm planning to cloister myself, meditate, swim, snorkel, walk, and reflect on things. Ben's looking forward to house-sitting for Delilah. And I'm wondering if you would mind taking emergency calls from my clients. No one's currently in crisis, and I'll let everyone know I'll be going away."

"That's fine. I'm always grateful when you do the same for me. But what about Sam?"

My heart sank into my stomach. I paused, gazing at the Catalinas, remembering our camping trips. "I'll write him a letter. He'll be in the field for another couple of weeks and won't return until November. I'll explain about Saul later; I'm not looking forward to that."

"I wouldn't be, either."

A dewy rain moistened my face as I climbed down the aluminum stairs at Hilo airport in the early evening. I felt embraced by the warmth and humidity while padding across the cement runway and into the air-conditioned terminal building. A flower stand adorned with leis attracted my eye. I approached, then asked the round-faced, elderly Hawaiian woman if she would put a garland on me as a gesture of welcome. I would buy it, of course. She laughed heartily and invited me to choose one.

I selected a bundle of yellow flowers mixed with orchids. She motioned for me to bend over and, smiling generously, hung the lei around my neck. Not knowing how to respond, I placed my hands in prayer position, bowed slightly, and thanked her.

She sat on her wooden chair and asked, "Now, what are you going to do first?"

I reached into my purse, pulled out the pencil sketch of directions to the Kalani Honua, and showed them to her.

She frowned. "It's not good to go down the red road at night. You stay in Hilo and go tomorrow."

I tucked the paper away and considered her suggestion. "I have a rented car," I said.

She patted me on the arm. "Okay, but you be careful. Don't stop for any reason till you get to that place."

"Welcome to paradise. I'm Judy," a young blond woman said as I approached the registration counter at the Kalani Honua. "Gwendolyn said to tell you she'll be back in a couple of days. She had some errands to run on the Kona side."

Judy led me across a meadow that, in the shadows, I could tell was surrounded by a wall of trees. My room was in one of the many screened-in wooden bungalows. "Tomorrow, when it's easier to see, you can park your car out here. Somebody's got the fire going in the sauna if you want to take one."

I hoisted my suitcase onto the low table at the foot of the single bed. "That would probably help my jet lag. Thanks."

The wooden sauna building was nestled among hibiscus, birds of paradise, and graceful ti bushes. Inside, a couple sat nude on a wooden bench, feeding the fire and splashing water on the hot rocks. I introduced myself and we chatted off and on. I then asked what they knew about the area. Carl shook his head, swinging his long curly hair, and said, "There's a private beach down the road— a cove only locals use. Kalapana, the famous black beach, is too touristy and dangerous for swimming. If you go down the road in the other direction and wind your way into the subdivision, you'll come to big lava pools completely protected from the waves. It's a great spot for snorkeling. And there's a little hot spring in the jungle. We can show you how to get to it."

I reached over to splash more water on the rocks. "A woman in the airport told me that the red road is dangerous at night. Do you know why?"

Carl leaned his wiry body against the redwood wall. "There's a legend about a battle that was waged here a long time ago. Some say spirits are still roaming around angry about what happened. They supposedly come out at night. Speaking of myths, you know about Pele, right?"

I nodded my head. "A little. I'd like to know more."

"She's the volcano goddess, and if she doesn't like what's going on down below she explodes, makes fireworks on the mountain, destroys houses, creates new landscapes—even new beaches! Once when she got angry, she sent down her lava flow, which burned to a crisp every house in the area but one—that of an old man who worshiped her. His house remained unscathed. There are a lot of stories like that. Some say Pele's mad now because of so many subdivisions, and that's why the lava's coming down there. Anyway, this side of the island is the one most prone to lava destruction. It's got more spirits too." Carl and Susan looked at each other and giggled.

It was Gwendolyn who had first told me about Pele, and based on what she said I had planned a morning drive to Kilauea to make an offering to the volcano in hopes that the goddess might bless my stay. After all, she seemed like a local form of the Mother.

Before breakfast, I hiked along the cliff bordering the ocean. The rusty-reddish road was bumpy, narrow, and paved with clay. Lining one side of it was a rain forest, and dotting the landscape between me and the water were banana and money-pod trees. I had strolled only a short distance when I noticed a school of dolphins jumping beyond the waves. A surge of joy spiraled through my body as I skipped to keep up with them. They scooted along parallel with me for quite a while, as if inviting me to frolic with them. *What a blessing it is to feel lighthearted after so much darkness.*

The retreat house served homemade rolls and hot cereal at a breakfast buffet in the dining hall. The lunch and evening meals consisted of fresh vegetables, salads, and tasty vegetarian dishes. The facility catered to various groups offering personal growth seminars or yoga retreats, as well as to private guests like me. Back from my early morning hike, I sat on the veranda eating a cinnamon roll and sipping coffee while gazing at the lush green terrain.

After winding my way up the mountain in my rental car, through abundant low-lying vegetation, I drove around Kilauea until I found a quiet place above the crater's steamy desolation where I could meditate. There I climbed out of the car clutching a plastic bag full of hibiscus flowers and sat on the edge of a cliff overlooking the flat, barren pit. One by one, I tossed the flowers over the edge, into an expansive abyss that could erupt at any time. I imagined Pele using the red blossoms to decorate her long black hair.

Kilauea was tumultuous. The sense of molten lava just beneath the earth's surface eliminated any illusion of security; the only certainty that remained for me was of an unalterable shifting governed by something much larger than myself. The active flow bubbling over the other edge of the volcano, as Carl and Susan had explained, slithered down the black rock mountain toward Kalapana Beach and the Kalani Honua. Even from where I was sitting it was clear that beneath the frail surface of the earth Pele slept, but not soundly. Aware that one heave of her breath could destroy everything in sight, I nevertheless mustered the courage to sit in a cross-legged position and close my eyes to meditate. As my gut writhed in rhythm with the churning of Pele's underground cauldron, I realized I had run away from emotional upheavals only to find the earth herself gyrating in a tempestuous dance. The shifts and eruptions, I concluded, must be among those natural states of creation the Mother spoke of. Then a question bubbled up: Could these states, as well as the constancy I'm seeking, be within *me?*

The next day Carl and Susan offered to accompany me—snorkeling gear and all—to the sites they had spoken of. After exploring the tide pools, the steam rising out of the sea where lava flowed into it, and the hot spring, I parked at the edge of a narrow pathway that switched back and forth down a cliff to the hidden cove. From there they returned to the Kalani Honua on foot while I hiked down to the cove.

Only a few people dotted the stretch of black sand, most of them in the nude. I slipped off my sarong, but kept on my bathing suit because of a nagging sense that someone was watching me. Glancing over my shoulder, I searched the cliff for signs of trouble. Nothing within my range of vision appeared suspect, although I did become aware of a buzzing in my ears. *This is new.*

Determined to avoid being victimized by pursuers, real or imagined, I shuffled through the volcanic sand, holding my fins, face mask, and snorkel. At the shoreline I put them on and stepped into the warm ocean. The bottom dropped off quickly, and suddenly I was treading water, gulping, sculling vigorously with my hands. After fixing my snorkel in place, I dipped under the surface to catch sight of the sand below, thinking it would help me feel more secure. Instead, I became engulfed in cobalt blue, fathomless and obscure, with no view of the ocean floor. Gradually, I settled into the primeval darkness, swam out some distance, then alternated between floating and treading water. As my body relaxed into the indigo swells, I could feel the Mother enveloping me in her oceanic womb.

On the horizon, which from my vantage point was rather close by, I saw flashes of gray. *Dolphins! I wonder if they will come.* I glided toward them, but they vanished around the edge of the cove. Whereas in mountains and deserts, the wolves, coyotes, and birds were my symbols of freedom and wild delight, in oceans they were dolphins. For years I'd dreamed of swimming with them, far from people burdened with fears and judgments, and apt to thwart my experience of unrestrained joy. *One day I'll find this happiness and it will never end, people or no people.*

Lying on my back, bobbing up and down like I did as a child in the tide pools at Whispering Sands Beach, I felt at home. Images of Sam sifted into my brain—our days and nights together before he left, bike rides in Saguaro National Monument, hikes through the washes with Delilah and Shaman. I sensed Sam floating next to me, easing in close and touching me. His warmth slipped inside of me, spinning and rolling like the dolphins.

Sometime later I raised my head, only to find that the beach had become a tiny speck in the distance. *The current must have been carrying me out to sea.* I splashed, racing toward shore, and quickly ran out of breath. *I'd better slow down.* I treaded water, then floated in drown-proofing style on my stomach—sinking down under, drifting up, taking a deep breath, and sinking down again. At last relaxed, I swam on a diagonal, like a sailboat tacking, and edged my way toward land. *My God, I must remember never to do this again.* As the current eased up, I found I could easily swim straight toward shore. Alternating between back stroke, side stroke, breast stroke, and drown proofing, I made my way in. All the while, the words of a song ran through my mind: "Mother, won't you carry me ashore . . ."

Once my toes touched the sand, I pulled off my fins, wove toward my towel, and slumped onto it, my heart beating wildly. Only one couple remained on the beach, suggesting that it was much later than I'd thought. *Once again I've gone astray.* In passionate moments, I'd tended to think actions had to be risky to succeed in following a dream. *Yes! Risky, but not stupid.* After I rested and dried, I pulled off my suit, slipped into my sarong, meditated for a while, then contemplated the orange glow on the water—a reflection cast by the sun setting not over the ocean, as it did in California, but rather behind me.

The next night Dave, a guide with shaggy, sun-bleached hair, took a few of us on a sight-seeing hike over freshly formed volcanic rock. We headed toward the area where steam rises out of the sea. In the moonlight we made our way through expanses of smooth black rock, like unpolished marble, and areas where the rocks aptly named *a'a* (ah-ah) in Hawaiian were pointed and sharp. Our guide's voice droned through his bushy mustache, cautioning us to follow in single file and be wary of where we stepped. Gingerly, we inched toward the active lava flow that had left newly formed land in its wake. I could feel the heat radiating through my thongs.

Dave explained how the fiery liquid had carved its course to the sea, destroying houses and vegetation in its wake. Before approaching the molten rock, he had us gather in a semicircle. "Some people, trying to get a better look, have slipped into the molten rock— and that was it for them. You have to be very careful here," he cautioned. "In places, the surface appears solid but is actually soft and extremely hot. Much hotter than what you're feeling right now. When the lava doesn't flow on the surface, it oozes underground through self-forming tubes. Later, the underground pathways harden into tunnel-like caves. A couple of you explored an inactive lava tube with me before dinner . . ."

I had been in the tube with Dave. By flashlight, we had stumbled over rocks and groped our way through a fifty-foot-wide opening. The tube curved underground for about seventy yards before coming out near the ocean. Now, the smell of sulfur let us know we were approaching the active site. From a safe distance we watched molten lava sizzle into steam as the massive river of red-orange earth poured into the sea.

By the fifth day, I knew the area well enough to be able to synchronize my spiritual disciplines with the rhythms surrounding me. Over lunch with Gwendolyn, I explained my need to explore and enjoy long hours alone. She laughed and said she promised not to worry about me. At that point I began waking up at five in the morning to meditate, drink juice or tea, take a forty-five minute walk, then meditate again. I would write in my notebook before lunch, which was either picnic style or in the dining room after hours. Later, I went snorkeling in the lake-size tide pools, or swimming and waiting for dolphins in the cove.

On one of my hikes, I wandered down a pathway through tree ferns, guavas, and wild orchids, then into the jungle, where I discovered a hot spring nobody seemed to know about. Each day after that I meditated there in the late afternoon, or walked to a bluff overlooking the sea to gaze at the sunset. Usually, I had dinner around seven o'clock, although sometimes I skipped it and ate only fruit. At night I bathed in the sauna, then meditated until ten or eleven.

Late one afternoon I hid my car near the pathway into the jungle and walked to the hot spring. Once there, I felt an uncustomary rumbling in the pit of my stomach. Yet the setting, as always, was idyllic: the small pool was nestled against rocks in a banana and fern tree forest spotted with stalks of ginger. A pair of keokeos fluttered their slate-colored wings, flashing white breasts and chasing each other among the trees. When I finished soaking, I felt an urge to stay and meditate until nightfall—a daring impulse, considering the spirits the Hawaiian elder in the airport had warned me about. Nevertheless, I decided that subjecting myself to them was not the same as inviting a Saul or a Sibyl into my home. Besides, by now I was easily able to bring to mind the Mother's image.

After meditating for a while, I felt something brush against my neck. I spun my head around, but saw nothing. Although my heart pounded and my breathing became erratic, I soon calmed down again. *If there are spirits here, they don't feel angry, as Carl and Susan suggested—just a bit unsettling.* Breathing deeply, I silenced my mind and floated into the soft humidity, the mossy smells, the caress of breezes, and the fragrance of the ginger plants.

Suddenly, what felt like two moist hands nudged my shoulders. This time my inner being was filled with such calm that when I turned and saw two brown-skinned men smiling, bearing torches, and clothed only in grass skirts and shell-and-seed necklaces, my body willingly rose to follow them into the forest. *If these men are phantoms, they seem very friendly and quite human.* We walked in single file through the lush and spongy jungle, one man in front of me and one behind. I began to wonder if I was dreaming. *If this is real, it's definitely bizarre.*

Still immersed in a state of calm, I felt no fear; on the contrary, sparkles of joy began to burst through my veins. *Maybe the Mother sent these men to help me find the immortal nectar.* After about a mile, we stopped at a thatched hut tucked under banana and papaya trees. There the men planted their flaming torches in the ground beside several others. They motioned me over to log hollowed into the shape of a chair and set in front of a bonfire. At this point I became a bit nervous, wondering what they had in store for me. *Maybe I should poke them gently to see if they're real.*

One by one, other men appeared, slipping though the trees as though through an opening in time. *Perhaps I've been transported into a past or future century.* A chubby native, belly rolling over his grass skirt, sat on a stump to play a kettle-shaped wooden drum. My two escorts stood like sentinels on either side of me as the others danced around the fire, their bare chests shining and shimmying. They wiggled their hips, undulated their torsos, the long narrow leaves of their ti plant skirts swishing, shells around their ankles rattling. One dancer brushed close to me, his eyes shining, tickling my knees with his grass skirt. *I feel that!* I wondered if it was possible to feel and still be in a dream.

The drums and dancing swept me into an ecstatic state. Soon a woman passed me a clay cup filled with warm white liquid. One of the dancers motioned for me to drink. My body trembled as I lifted the mug to my lips and sipped. I paused, suddenly suspicious, but too nervous not to do as they requested. The drums continued beating as skirts flashed around and around. In the blur of my growing confusion, I saw my two attendants standing in front of me, smiling and apparently waiting for me to finish the last drop of the sweet, slightly bitter, thick and lumpy liquid. After that, I do not know what happened.

Sometime later, I woke in a dark place. Covered with a lightweight cloth, I was lying on what felt like sealskin, smooth and flat. My head was as clear as a pool in the jungle and my heart was quiet. Although curious about where I was, I still believed the Mother might have been behind this mystery, hence I trusted that whoever had brought me here would eventually come to fetch me. I crawled around, probing with my hands, then realized I was probably in a lava tube. It smelled dank, like a cave, and echoed sharply when I called out, "Ha! Yo! Anyone here?" Hearing no answer, I was struck by the thought that I might have been drugged and brought here against my will. A wave of foreboding rolled over me in the muted silence. *Why did they bring me here?*

Cautiously, I headed back to the skin bed, bumping into a clay water jug on the way. After smelling its contents, I poured a few drops on my tongue. The liquid was cool and fresh, as if from a spring. Taking some more steps, I came upon a basket of fruit and a ceramic bowl containing a sticky mixture. I licked the sweet paste and, at a loss for anything else to do, wrapped the cloth around my shoulders and sat on the skin to meditate. My thoughts wandered back to the dancing men and their bittersweet drink, which I realized may have been a calming elixir for my stay in the darkness.

As time passed, I began to feel restless and unable to sustain a connection to the Mother. My thoughts wandered to alligators in jungle rivers, bats swarming out of caves, masses of beetles clustering around my bare feet. *I'd better remember to breathe.* But even slow, deep inhalations and exhalations did nothing to alleviate my increasing fear. I opened my eyes and, seeing only a wall of darkness, felt an urge to run and release the scream that bubbled in the chambered nautilus of my belly. *I must stay calm.*

All at once, I was startled by a loud buzzing in my ears, whirring at a much higher decibel than the one I'd heard at the black-sand beach. A moment later, I saw Kilauea in full eruption. The volcano burned my insides and blazed at my temples, giving way to rolling drops of sweat. *If this is the underworld, it's far more horrifying than I've ever imagined.* I flashed onto my Gestalt session and Chaser's description of himself as the "faceless dark" and "terror of the unknown." *This may well be what he was referring to.* Throwing myself onto the sealskin, I tossed my head and body from side to side, then sang over and over again, "In the still of the night, from the darkness comes the light, and I know in my heart it is you," until I was hoarse and exhausted.

I must have dropped off to sleep, for the next thing I knew I was staring into an infernal darkness in which time had lost all meaning.

To temper the heat burning inside me, I took more sips of water and munched on a papaya from the basket, refraining from the sticky stuff for fear that it may have caused my fiery visions. I breathed deeply and whispered, "Show me the daylight," again and again. Shifting around on the sealskin, I twisted my body back and forth to shake loose what I still hoped was only a dream.

Visions of the Kilauea fireworks display, however, persisted. *I must try to just watch it and see what comes next.* Surprisingly, I was able to observe it with my mind, which somehow hovered slightly above and behind me. *So, this is a way to be detached from my mind and body!* Now a witness rather than a participant, I was thrilled by the sight. However, I soon became aware of a blistering in the pit of my stomach from which I could not detach—a hell that plagued me with a shivering terror, as though I myself had plummeted into that underworld of fire. I tried to escape by lying down, but the smoldering persisted. I shook my fists. I cried out, "Mother! Where are you? Ma!" Seeing no signs of her, I was certain she had abandoned me and I would die in darkness. At last I collapsed into the dead silence.

When I came to, I heard what sounded like a slow drip echoing from far away. *Maybe I can get out of here on my own.* I moved cautiously, groping hand over hand along the cave wall, my bare feet stumbling on stones. Fortunately, there were no *a'a* lava rock formations, only smooth ones—though these, too, were sometimes precipitous. Arriving at a spot where the floor of the cave zigzagged downward, I was afraid to go farther. *At least I have food back there.* I edged my way back, crawling like a crab.

Hungry for something other than fruit, and convinced that my visions were not a result of the sticky stuff, I swallowed several fingerfuls of it and felt somewhat nourished and pacified. A scalding sensation in my stomach, however, soon gripped me and began inching its way into my chest and throat. I clasped my neck to ease the heat that singed my nerves. Contemplating the blackness, I began whispering the refrain "From the darkness comes the light . . ." *Mother, please, isn't this enough? Must I be burned and tortured in your underworld?*

After a while, I glimpsed a spot of light in the distance, at first only a pinprick, then larger and bubbling. Thinking it was someone who had come to lead me out, I jumped and waved wildly, hoping the beam of their flashlight would catch the movement of my arms. Then I froze, opening and closing my eyes in disbelief. The light grew bigger and bigger till all at once I was assaulted by flying flames and a demon-like creature with fangs, flaring nostrils, and shaggy hair. I ducked and flattened onto the sealskin. With the fibers of my being stretched like threads ready to snap, I emitted a pitiful squeak in the reverberating dankness, "Please, somebody, save me." Then, supposing the mother of this island would like to hear her name, I called aloud to the volcano goddess, "Pele, are you there?" I heard nothing but a damp echo and, in my mind, blazes from the infernal fire.

Twirling around and around in place, I murmured, "Pele, Pele," whereupon my hand bumped against the water jug. I lifted it and gulped, spilling the cool liquid down the front of my sarong. Again the demon swished past me, this time knocking the pot to the ground. The creature's green eyes rolled as it blew hot air into my face. Sweat poured. Probing with my feet, I backed up against the cave wall, flailing my arms, crying, "Pele, please cast this demon into your lava pit!"

The volcano gushing inside my brain turned the flying beast into a crackling fireball. I screamed, "Pele! Mother!" Only silence. This time the demon flew at me roaring like a bonfire, its face contorted, with pointed chin and dimples. *Saul!* I clamped my hands to my face and swung back and forth. At that moment the thing, still with traces of Saul's features, raised its huge pale hands, now ablaze above its head, and brought them slowly down toward my neck. I slumped to the ground, curled up on my knees, and with my hands in prayer position, murmured, "Mother, take me to you." Then I collapsed.

Something or someone lifted my head. Raising my aching eyelids, I gazed, awestruck, at Pele, with long black hair and a red gown, hovering behind the sparks of the eruption, arms spread in welcome. She smiled at me, then formed her mouth into a cavernous hole. The demon, face crooked and gnarled, roared and flew at me again, but was sucked into the fiery crater of her mouth. She drew him in and spit him back out, burning, twisting, writhing until he was nothing but a wisp of floating ash, white and glowing amid the flames. Then she, too, vanished.

I rose to my knees and wept, "Mother, thank you!" Enveloped in love within the cave's warm silence, my body softened, limber and moist. Embraced by darkness, I closed my eyes and began to sing, softly at first, then in full voice: "In my heart I hear you calling . . . You are holding my destiny . . . On the path to eternal freedom . . . you mean everything to me."

After a while, I began to burst with laughter, rolling on the sealskin until my belly ached. *So that's it! I am creation—good and evil.* I could see that the dream chasers, the bushman, Sibyl, Saul, and the dark side of my father were all expressions of my own sordid nature. When Pele swallowed the demon, it was the evil in *me* that had turned to ashes. Now, with no judgments and no attachments, even to the notion of benevolent or wicked, I was free.

For some time I lay in the ecstasy of deliverance, filled with soothing images of fountains, keokeos, hibiscus flowers, and banana trees. Gradually, everything in the interior of the cave was warmed in light. I bathed in the glow, in the blank slate of my mind, in what seemed a never-ending peace.

When thirst and hunger nagged, I was struck once more by my predicament. *I must eat and get out of here.* Sitting hunched over, I nibbled on a mango and sucked on the mixture, all the while aware that my sense of well-being was stronger than my worries. Then sleep took me, and I began to fade into and out of a lullaby of dreams, seeing images of Sam smiling, ebbing into an ocean of love.

The next thing I knew, I was blindfolded, yet could see light through the cloth, hear the sound of waves, and smell salt from the sea. *Where are they taking me now?* Someone led me barefoot into the water, set me floating on my back, then slipped the blindfold from my eyes. Staring about, I was delighted to have been released from the agonies of that underworld horror, and oddly grateful to them, for without the dim underworld I'd never have known such clarity. I splashed through the water, then rolled over, squinting in the uncustomary brightness to catch a glimpse of my deliverer—but whoever it was had vanished. *It must have been the Mother. Perhaps she dove beneath the surface, or swam behind a rock.* My heart hammered in my chest as I scanned the water. "Mother!" I called, but she didn't appear.

The sun's early morning rays sparkled more brightly on the surface of the sea. I floated on swells of rapture, singing, "Deep inside I long to tell you . . . you mean everything to me." Brimming over with delight, I spotted a sea turtle a few feet away, then a school of shimmering yellow fish with black stripes. A reef beneath me was apparently a hiding place for sea creatures. Stepping onto a nearby rock, I stood waist-deep in the water, swaying to and fro with the rise and fall of waves as I surveyed the area. The land beyond the beach looked like a site near the lava tube I had explored with Dave, not far from the red road. *I'll have to figure all this out later.*

I dove in, rolled in the lapping waves, paddling and splashing until suddenly something bumped me from behind. Then it nudged me to the surface, turned me loose, and undulated in and out of the water, splashing in circles around me. *A dolphin!* Gliding by, it grazed my skin, reminding me of the sensation I'd had while touching the coyote. I moved swiftly to keep up with the dolphin, lost it, and began treading water. Once again, it brushed against me, this time letting me paddle alongside it, rolling and turning in the swells as I imitated its movements.

Finally, my new friend rested perfectly still, gazing into my eyes. I had heard that dolphins communicate in rays of pure energy; and indeed, this one seemed to be saying, "I am love—pure, abandoned love." Feeling a rush of ecstasy stream through me, I swirled through the turquoise luminescence. But by the time I surfaced, the dolphin had disappeared, leaving me with an openheartedness I'd felt only with the Mother, Sam, and the coyotes.

After curling and winding through the water for a while, I stroked hard and fast to catch a small wave, and rode it to shore. Prancing out of the water, I spun around on the beach, then fell onto the warm sand. With a sudden burst of self-consciousness, I realized I was completely nude. Rolling over onto all fours, I looked up and down the beach, wondering how I was going to get back to the Kalani Honua without my clothes. Fortunately, not a soul was in sight—not even a car. Then on some rocks under a tree, I noticed a pile of clothes neatly folded and stacked. I scurried over, happy to find my thongs, sarong, shoulder bag, and the towel I had sat on at the spring. While slipping my sarong over my head, I heard a loud splash. *The dolphin!* But when

I turned, there was the Mother, knee-deep in the water, wet robes clinging to her body, and dolphins breaking in the distance.

I skipped over to her and stopped short, painting her image in my mind, imprinting it into my brain to keep it there forever. She chuckled, then took my hand and led me down the beach to a palm tree, where we sat facing the sea.

"Child, you have learned something about the fire of spiritual discipline, and the burning of negativities that hide your true nature."

A chill ran through me, and I nodded.

"And then you tasted a small drop of immortal nectar, did you not?"

I smiled, raised my knees, rested my chin on them, recalling the inner light, and my swim with the dolphin. Then my mind turned a corner, flashing onto memories of the demon and the erupting volcano. To affirm my new understanding, I asked, "Mother, are you Pele too?"

She remained silent, watching the dolphins that had come closer to shore and were leaping in and out of the waves. I remembered the Mother telling me of the many aspects of herself at our last meeting. Curious, I wondered if she'd now reveal that she was the dolphins and also the demon.

"Daughter, I am the essence of all things. I am the Hawaiian woman who welcomed you at the airport; I am the lava flow pouring into the ocean; I am the hurricane at sea and the watery moon. I am the dew from the rains, and the dolphins playing in the waves. When you pray to the river, or the trees, or the volcano, you are praying to me. Do not become deluded into thinking one thing is separate from another. The opposite shore seems separated from us by water, but if the ocean were to dry up, we would plainly see there is one continuous stretch of land."

Her words filled me with a love that gushed out like thousands of shooting stars, yet at the same time I felt soft and peaceful. I wondered what part she'd played in my experience in the cave, and if she was assisted by the men from another time, if that was in fact the truth about them.

"Do not try to hold on to a thing, child. Everything will come to you in its own time."

I frowned and drew my finger through the sand. "I'm having difficulty feeling sure I comprehend what all this means."

The Mother giggled. "What is it that binds everything together? It is love. It is the pure, unselfish heart flowing freely, offering itself without expectations."

Erasing my lines in the sand, I etched a big circle and looked at her out of the corners of my eyes. "How I can remain that way always?"

Her eyes reflected the sun on ocean swells. "Do not stop in your efforts. In time you will come to know me completely. Then you will be with me all the time." She kissed my cheek, pulled my head to her breast, held me for a while. Then she rose, floated across the sand, dipped into the waves, and swam like a fish to the school of dolphins, which frolicked alongside her as she glided toward the horizon and disappeared into the sea.

My heart sank, for I wanted her with me eternally. I strolled to the edge of the water and dug my big toe into the sand, holding my sarong up to let the waves splash my legs. How many times must she come and go, I wondered, before the immortal nectar flows through me? She'd hinted that this divine honey had to do with unconditional love, which I experienced firsthand during my three-day retreat back in Tucson. But I was not yet acquainted with the sense of nonseparation, even though I realized that must have been what I'd glimpsed in the cave and while floating in the ocean.

I imagined the ocean bottom leading to another shore, with the sea forging only the *appearance* of division. I yearned more than anything to be with this woman forever; yet curiously, this anguished longing seeded my heart with joy. Turning, I shuffled through the pumiced grains of shells and sat with my back against the tree. There I felt my mind expand into the sky and across the ocean waters.

After a while, I became aware of an unfamiliar form of observing— one similar to, yet stronger than, what I'd experienced in the cave when my mind was watching the fire from a point slightly above and behind my head. Viewing my surroundings in this way now, I felt no sense of separation. I twisted and turned in the sand, and still nothing disrupted my sense that the tree was me, as was the ground and the tropical breeze, the salty humid smell, the sound of the waves rushing to shore and licking the grains of sand. The outside and inside of me were *one and the same*.

Chapter Eight

The All-Devouring Universe

The landscape was brilliant as a meadow after the lifting of morning mist, as I walked down the red road back to my car. I seemed to occupy a vacant body, to gaze through eyes not my own at crisp, luminous colors splashed onto nature's canvas. Gingerly, I stepped along the red clay, cherishing it as a part of my body. It was as though my mind had blended with all things. I still saw trees as trees, ocean as ocean, me as me, in the same way I always had, yet I was perceiving them with a renewed love for everything.

At the Kalani Honua I parked the car behind my bungalow and strolled to my room. In the bathroom mirror I noticed that my face had changed considerably, even more than it had upon my return from the Chiricahuas. Now my long, tangled hair framed softened features. My eyes were brighter, more blue-green than gray. After combing out the knots of hair as best I could, I showered, then meandered over to the dining hall.

Along the way, Judy stopped me. "Sam called. Nobody knew where you were."

My brain swirled. "Sam?" *My God, how did he know to call here?* I struggled for words.

Judy smiled. "He sounded nice. Said he'll try again this afternoon at four."

My mind waded through mud. I looked at my watch, hoping it would help me get oriented, but after a long pause I had to ask, "Do you know what day it is?"

Judy laughed. "Everyone loses time here. It's Wednesday."

I was gone for two nights. Nodding, I thanked her and ambled down the path to the dining hall, absorbed once more in my new perception of the world—the brilliant greens of the trees and grass, the pulsing orange of the birds of paradise. Even the thud of my flip-flops bumping up the wooden stairs and the squeaking of the screen door caused rushes of joy to ripple through me. Then spurts of worry began to break through my serenity. Was Sam concerned about me? Had he found out about my encounter with Saul? As if giving up the struggle to revive its pestering thoughts, my mind immediately released its agitation, merging as before into the beauty and wonder of the surroundings.

Janet, the woman behind the lunch buffet, said, "Luce, you look happy. Where have you been?"

My words were trapped in a well of silence. I laughed. "I went on a little adventure." My eyes wandered over the lavish spread. My cave diet had left me with such a delicate feeling in my stomach that it was difficult to select from among the many casseroles, salads, and desserts.

Janet handed me a glass of iced peppermint tea and, with a twinkle in her eye, asked, "Did you find a Hawaiian lover?"

"Sort of."

A hoarse giggle bubbled from her plump belly. "We make picnic lunches, you know. Next time, tell us when you go off like that."

"You can be sure I will." I stared at the generous display of food, and finally settled on a banana smoothie and a mango salad.

I savored the meal on the veranda, then rested in the embrace of island sweetness, sometimes dozing, sometimes enchanted by the jungle sounds, the dew dripping, the ground pulsing with invisible life.

As the afternoon wore on, I flashed back to my time in the lava tube, so black and utterly terrifying. By contrast, my emergence into light had awakened unimaginable feelings of peace and exaltation. But who were those men in grass skirts? Had I in fact slipped into another time? Had the Mother actually been involved in my kidnapping? No matter how the fiery encounter had been orchestrated, I was relieved to know that my difficulties with Sibyl and Saul had originated in the darkness of my own mind, and that the fire of Pele's volcano had burned away something in me, some inner sticky stuff that kept attracting negative thoughts and feelings.

Suddenly, Judy peeked around the open door to tell me Sam was on the line. My stomach tightened as I raced inside.

"God, Luce, what're you doing in Hawaii?"

I leaned forward on the wooden chair behind the reception counter. Even though I'd felt Sam with me during some of my adventures, at the moment he seemed remote. "It's hard to talk here. I'm on a public phone, and there's too much to tell you."

"You sound distant."

I fiddled with the cord and felt my heart shut itself into a little iron cage. "Everything's okay now. There were some difficulties and I had to get away."

"I was dying to see you, so I asked for a long weekend off. I've been having incredible dreams about you. I wanted to surprise you, so I bought a ticket to fly to Tucson tomorrow, but something told me I'd better call first."

My heart jumped into my throat. *How am I going to talk to him?* "I get back Sunday—can you wait? Do you want to pick me up at the airport?"

"Sure. I'm not due to return to the wilderness program until Monday night. What happened, anyway? Are you okay?"

"I really am okay. I miss you, too."

Back in Tucson, I searched through a sea of faces as I stepped into the airport waiting room. Sam pushed through the crowd and grabbed me, enfolding me against his bulky chest. I melted into him, feeling the same exhilaration I had while swimming with him in my imagination at the black-sand beach. Neither one of us could speak; we could only smile and look into each other's eyes. He took my hand and pulled me toward the baggage claim. As we wove through swarms of people, fear gnawed at me like locusts. *How will he react to my involvement with Saul?* He had always been understanding, but something told me he wouldn't be this time.

Sam stopped, held my face in his hands, and kissed my forehead. "You look more lovely than ever."

I felt a rush of heat flash across my face. Slipping my arm around his waist, I nudged him forward. "Don't make me blush."

His nose wrinkled with joy as he swung his hips into mine. "You're pretty when you blush. Come on, what's wrong with you?"

"Jet lag, I guess. And I do have a long story to tell."

Almost imperceptibly, his hand shifted on my shoulder, revealing a sinking and tensing of muscles. "That sounds ominous."

Sam had stopped at the natural food store for a picnic lunch of gourmet take-outs in Sabino Canyon. Arriving in the canyon, we strolled along the stream and found a grassy spot in a grove of cottonwoods on the other side of the water, secluded from Sunday visitors. At the base of a huge tree, Sam spread the blanket he'd brought and pulled me onto it. "I've been dying to lie next to you," he said. "Maybe we should have gone home first." We touched and caressed and held each other, merging with the sounds of sparrows, the gurgling of the stream, and the occasional chatting of people strolling by.

Yearning welled up within me, but I pulled away, leaned on my elbow, and ran my fingers through his hair. A sense of foreboding lurked at the bottom of my stomach like an eel in an underwater crevice. "It's almost like we have to get to know each other again. It's been a long time, Sam. So much has happened in the five months you've been gone."

I started to reach for the food, but he pulled me on top of him and tickled my neck with his lips. "Ah, the artfulness of suspense," he replied. Then he rolled away, ripped open the food sack, chewed off the end of the French loaf, and dug into the Greek salad. As we ate, he told me about the wilderness project. "Most of the prisoners came away feeling less caged, less trapped by their circumstances. I think it's going to become part of the program for many prisons. You're smiling. You're happy about it, huh? You won't have to listen to me complaining anymore, right?"

My heart melted. He looked so familiar, as if I'd known him all my life. I moved closer, took his hand, held his palm to my lips, and looked into his eyes.

He gently pressed his forehead against mine. "Now, enough of me. So what happened that drove you to Hawaii?" He stretched out his legs and leaned against the tree.

I felt deep remorse, and knew I must tell him regardless of the consequences. I massaged his calf. "Please remember this: You are the most important person in my life. My love for you grows and grows. You know that, don't you?"

He pulled his leg away, drew his knee up to his chest. "Come on, what happened?"

My body turned cold and damp as I spoke. In the worst, most seductive parts I had to clench my teeth to stop them from chattering. Although I could feel Sam squeezing inwardly as the story of Saul progressed, he sat quietly through the entire account. At the end, he picked up a stick, stood, and broke it into small pieces, throwing them in different directions. "So what're we supposed to do now?"

My stomach tightened. "I was hoping we could get through this."

He kicked the tree and paced. "What do you think I am—some sort of teddy bear you can just play around with?"

I knew it was my turn to be compassionate, but at the moment it seemed impossible to give him the empathy he had so often given me. My voice quivered. "Oh, Sam. I've said I'm sorry."

He grabbed a dead branch and smashed it against the tree, shattering the limb. "Am I supposed to believe all that Hawaii nonsense?"

The branch broke something inside of me. I slumped forward into a black hole and rocked back and forth. Icicles stabbed me from all sides. *Oh God, please help me.* "Sam, I love you. Just tell me what I have to do so you'll forgive me."

"Well, for starters, I'm going for a walk. I'll see you at your house tonight." He reached in his pocket, pulled out the car keys, threw them onto the blanket, and stomped off.

I ran after him. "How will you get home?"

Sprinting away from me, he yelled, "That part's easy."

I waded into the stream with my shoes on, my heart beating wildly. "I want to know about the dreams you had. Sam!" I hung my head. *Oh, Mother, where are you now?* I shuffled back to the blanket and, like a robot, stuffed the leftovers into Sam's day pack, slinging it over my shoulder. I meandered down the trail to the parking lot, my head spinning, empty, numb.

Delilah was moping in a corner, as she usually did after missing me for a few days. "I'm sorry, girl. I've let you down, too. Come on, let's go for a walk." She brushed her tail reluctantly against the floor, then edged toward me, head down. The late September sky reflected my frame of mind: black thunderheads spread across the horizon, darkening the afternoon sky to an unusual degree.

As Delilah and I traipsed through the wash, lightning flashed and thunder sounded. I yelled into the storm, "Sam, give me another chance. I know you're hurt. We can get through this!" Huge drops of rain pelted my face while I plodded on, welcoming the distraction from my pain. Thunder roared deafeningly seconds after a blinding flash of light. Sheets of water soaked us to the skin. Then—*crack!*— a shaft of lightning crashed into a mesquite tree, slashing one of its limbs. I belly-flopped onto the sand and held Delilah close. She shivered and shook. The rain beat in pellets. "We'll be okay, girl. Just lie still." Now another streak flashed—*bang!*— from behind. A swoosh of leaves and limbs smashed as the water in the wash rose around us.

After a few minutes, the thunder and lightning eased, but the rain was relentless. Nestled with Delilah against a fortress of branches, I lifted my head to survey the damage and was astonished to see two large mesquite limbs split off from their trunks like twigs. *My God, we're lucky we weren't killed . . . It's the Mother again!* Now I held my face to the sky, kneeling in water that was rapidly climbing to my thighs. "Mother!" Delilah had scampered to the bank, barking at me to cease this nonsense and climb to safety. I closed my eyes and prayed, "Mother, please help me understand who you are. You saved us from this storm, but are you the lightning too? And the beloved? If it is in your power, please forgive me and set me free. Do you hear me? Let this water from your sky wash me clean. Let me bathe in your love forever and ever!" I bowed my head, wet hair dripping down my face.

Then I rose and waded toward the bank, nearly tumbling over from the force of the rushing water. *Give me some sign, Mother, that you've heard my prayer.* Soon the cloudburst let up and a shaft of light beamed through, outlining the clouds with a golden halo. I raised my arms, calling to the sky, "Thank you!"

Shivering with cold, I climbed onto the bank and contemplated the storm's wake. How perfectly it reflected my own state of being! My shaggy dog bounded over, wagging her tail, then licking my face as she shook, spraying water all about us. Prancing, she threw her head to one side and rolled her eyes—a signal I recognized as her plea to go home. "Okay, girl, let's go."

As we strolled along beside the wash, I was in awe of the river gushing through the usually dry bed, carrying all manner of sticks and leaves, carving the banks anew. The celestial timpani still rumbled in the distance. Although my heart ached, I felt cleansed, and hopeful that nature's purification ritual would help Sam and me mend.

In the temple room I lit several candles and bunched together a pile of pillows, then flopped down and waited for Sam. I lay still, listening to my heart beat and feeling the blood rush through my brain. After what felt like hours but was actually only two minutes, I made tea, then sang along with a tape, winding it back to the same piece over and over again: "Teach me the language of your heart . . ." I desperately hoped the words of this song would become my own when I faced Sam.

Finally, there was a knock at the door. I tried to get up, but my knees wobbled and my legs felt like putty. I crawled to the entryway, where I reached for the doorknob and pulled myself up. *Sam, please be okay.* I opened the door and sunk into him without even looking at his face. I clung to his waist. "Are you all right?"

He held his arms lightly around me, then we shuffled into the temple room and fell onto the pillows. The frown line across his forehead was deep. "We have to talk."

I folded my hands, knuckles white, and held them tightly to my chest. "Are you hungry? Do you want some tea?"

He cleared his throat. "How about some tea and cinnamon toast."

When I came back with the tray, he looked the same—like a man returned from a long journey, a crusade, perhaps a quest. Only after eating did he break his long silence. "Here's the deal, plain and simple. I love you more than I realized. If we're going to continue, I need to know I can trust you. Always. Until death do us part."

Oh, thank you, Mother. Leaning forward, I touched his hand. "I . . ."

He pulled away. "I'm not finished speaking."

Even without looking at him I could feel his eyes drilling into me. Fear of losing his love flooded over me, but I tried not to show it. I wanted to reflect compassion for *him*, rather than concern for *me*.

"I really got my buttons pushed over this Saul thing. I already had one woman leave me for another man. But I never suspected you would, too. If this is going to work out, we'll have to go to counseling together, or something like that."

Perched on my knees, I let out the breath I'd been holding. "I'd . . ."

"Wait, I did a lot of thinking in that storm out in Sabino Canyon. I'm still not finished."

I pinched my lips together and nodded vigorously, pointing to myself as if to say, "Me too."

Sam almost cracked a smile, then cast his gaze downward and frowned. "So, this is the second part of the idea. When I get back, I want to train you for a week-long vision quest. We could go to the Colorado mountains, or maybe somewhere in the desert—that is, *if* we can work things out through counseling. A vision quest might cement us together in a way that's important to me, beyond the normal couple thing. But first I need to know I can trust you."

I folded my arms against my chest to hold back the explosion in my heart, now swollen with love. "It won't happen ever again. I promise. I love you, Sam."

He grinned, unclasped my fingers, and kissed them, then held them to his cheek.

I snuggled up against him. "I'm actually glad you got so angry; it let me know the measure of your love for me, and of mine for you. It's painful, I can tell, but I think this experience will deepen our relationship far beyond our expectations."

"It already has," he said as we stretched out on the pillows. He touched his mouth to my forehead, and we stayed like that for a long time, lying very still, with only the pulse of blood throbbing through our bodies, melting like lava, burning. We floated into one-ness as if we were eagles riding the winds of desert canyons, then soaring into the mountains and beyond.

The next day I saw clients all morning and found it surprising-ly easy to focus. I even felt more effective than usual, probably because I was in touch with more aspects of my own nature and able to accept both the good and the bad in myself and others. Sam knocked on the door about three o'clock, waking me from a nap. We sauntered onto the porch arm in arm. "I've been hiking on Pima Canyon Trail," he said. "It became really clear that we've got to start our vision quest training as soon as I get back."

"No counseling first?" I flopped down on the old chaise lounge.

"We can do that on weekdays and the trainings on weekends. Listen, I've got a dream to tell you." He dragged over another lounge chair and sat, leaning forward, eyes open and round. "I was burning like that volcano when you revealed your rendezvous with Saul. I was so enraged, there was no way I was going to share how close to you I'd been feeling. Actually, I lied when I said the Hawaii stuff was nonsense. The week before you were there, while I was still in San Francisco, I had a dream showing the exact details of your experience in the cave."

Rushes of energy ran up my spine. I rolled onto Sam's lounge chair, pushing him down, and nuzzled against his chest as his arms closed around me. The whirring of a hummingbird sounded nearby, then I felt the Mother holding our heads to her breast. I closed my eyes to feel a more vivid sense of union with him. After a while Sam said something, but I didn't hear his words. Moments later I vaguely felt him tapping me on the back. Then he shook me, startling me out of my reverie, whereupon I whispered. "The Mother is blessing us. Can you feel it?"

I felt his muscles tense. "That Mother stuff is yours, not mine."

I squeezed his hand and rolled back onto my lounge chair. "Mmm, we might have to share our trainings when you get back. We'll meet halfway. After all, if I'm going to be with her forever, I want you there, too."

He folded his arms across his chest. "Come on, Luce. You can't *train* me in something like that. It has to just happen, doesn't it?"

I sat up cross-legged and leaned forward. "Meditation would be a start. Are you willing to try it?"

He smacked his lips and looked at his watch. "Give me a chance to think about it."

One morning after Sam had returned to the Bay Area, I awoke from a frightening dream not knowing where I was. It must have been very early, because stars still dotted a black sky. I peered around my bedroom, half expecting the lion from my dream to be lurking in the shadows. Moments before, Sam and I had been perched on a boulder in a meadow, contemplating the stars, when a mountain lion came down from a constellation and circled us by the light of the full moon. We watched it prowl, closer and closer, until I woke up. After all I'd been through, was I still not free of Antonio and his jaguar ceremony?

On another night, I dreamed of Sam and me climbing a snow-peaked mountain and playing in a meadow amid a chorus of larks, warblers, and hummingbirds. As we were entwined in each other's arms, his lips pressed against my forehead and I saw rainbows arcing over us.

Over the next few nights, the Mother entered my dreams, her image at first dim and distant, her features unclear. Then the contours sharpened, at which point she seemed to have many arms and to be dressed in colorful garments with flashes of reds and metallics. She was holding objects too faint for me to identify. Sometimes she danced, whirling around, the articles in her hands catching the light and shimmering like gold.

Our first vision quest took place beside a stream in the eastern portion of the Chiricahuas one weekend in mid-November. There Sam taught me about the Four Corners region and how to build a sacred circle of rocks and pray to each direction, including the earth and sky. He said the symbolism varied from culture to culture. "For our purposes, north is the warrior, south the child, west the ancestors, and east the visionary. The sky is the father, and the earth the mother. We might even discover our animal guides—special creatures who will teach us about the physical and spirit worlds."

"Like the wolf and coyote?" I asked. "I've sure learned from them."

"Yeah, like that—only don't get stuck on one idea about what they mean."

"What more could I want than to have them teach me about myself, lead me to the Mother, and bring me closer to you?"

Sam grabbed a stick and snapped it in two. "Just be open, Luce. And here's something else, although it's not based on traditional wisdom: You'll always be safe inside the circle if you urinate in various places a few yards from its circumference. Coyotes, mountain lions, and other large animals will regard this space as your territory; they'll walk around it like a fence. I've seen this happen."

Then he taught me how to be invisible by smearing my face with mud and hiding in grasses or bushes. He said it wasn't needed for a vision quest, but was good training in how to stay quiet, especially if I wanted to observe animals. We practiced it just for fun, washing off in the stream afterward. One time he hid so well that I couldn't find him even though he was sending me grunting and growling clues. When he leapt out of the grasses just a few feet from me, I shrieked in surprise.

We spent the first night together and the second night out of each other's sight in our own lean-tos. Sam had helped me make mine. We'd suspended a pole between the forked branches of two Gambel oaks, lashed them with twine, then set about preparing the latticework with an opening facing south, and insulating it with layers of needles and leaves. If I needed more warmth, I was to make a small fire-pit—a shallow hole lined with rock—just outside the opening to the shelter. Although water was allowed, we were not to eat until our time alone was over. Then Sam explained the buddy system and how we would have an agreed-upon location for checking in with each other, once in late morning and again in late afternoon. To show that we'd been there, we were to leave a little castle of rocks or another obvious sign. If we arrived at the spot and saw no sign, we were to go to the other's site and be prepared to help with first aid.

We'd also agreed to practice "tuning in" to each other—something our dreams suggested was indeed possible. In our sacred circles we would each keep an article of clothing from the other—a shirt, sock, or hat—which we were to check a couple of times a day. While touching it and closing our eyes, we would await an image or a message.

At noon on Sunday we met at the base camp, where we had pitched a tent. By the time I arrived, Sam had already made coffee and was cooking oatmeal over the fire. "So, how was it?" he asked.

I wrapped my arms around him from the back and leaned my head on his shoulder. "After getting over missing you, it was great—quiet and peaceful. I heard coyotes and saw a couple of deer. I felt the Mother the whole time, although I never saw her. She felt loving and warm as I prayed to the south. In the north, she was stern, like a chief disciplining a brave; I'd never seen that side of her. In the west, she came out of the ocean like Venus, and my ancestors were surrounding her. In the east, I felt peace and I meditated with her for a long time. At nightfall I stargazed for a few minutes, and then fell asleep. How about you?"

Sam handed me a bowl of oatmeal and some coffee. "It was a little weird. I dreamed about your mountain lion. It felt ominous, but when I checked in with your shirt, everything seemed fine."

My stomach contracted a little. "There *are* mountain lions up here, aren't there?"

Sam picked up a couple of stones and tossed them at a large rock, sometimes hitting it, sometimes missing. "Yeah, but there's nothing to worry about unless you provoke them by running or by dripping blood. Oh, one more thing: don't form a heart with the rocks. We're supposed to leave only a marker—an unemotional sign."

I laughed. "Okay, I won't do it again. Your shirt felt so good that I wanted to let you know it."

He threw a stone overhand and hit a tree. "You're supposed to touch my clothes only to check in. For a vision quest you have to be a little more detached. How are we going to get our visions if all we think about is each other? Remember, Luce, vision questing is as profound for me as being with the Mother is for you."

I scraped the bottom of my cereal bowl. "Maybe our visions will be about each other. Or maybe the Mother will come to you too."

He stood up and washed his dish, using the water we'd brought in gallon jugs. "There's no way we can know what it'll be."

I wondered why he seemed so tense. "What happened last night?"

"Nothing. Just that dream."

"Sam, have you ever had visions on one of these quests?"

"No visions yet, just incredible peace and feelings of oneness with nature. I'm counting on our week-long quest to bring me a vision, hopefully through an animal guide that will transport me between this world and others. I can feel it coming, you know what I mean?"

December and January were too cold for more training, although we did begin counseling, which seemed to help us with the Saul problem. In counseling I discovered more ways in which the absence of my father had impaired my trust in male-female relationships. For one, I became highly aware of my fear of abandonment—a dread that may have caused me to turn to Saul in Sam's absence. I saw, too, that I'd stopped obsessing over my father's seedy nature and begun instead to appreciate the tenderness he showered me with while swimming in the ocean together or walking in the woods. Sam realized that as the youngest of five boys he had missed out on closeness with his mother. As a result, he was extremely sensitive to anything that threatened to intrude on his closeness with me.

We also examined sexuality. Our exquisite lovemaking before Sam's six-month absence, I learned, had left my body aching for more human touch. Saul's advances further stimulated that craving—a reality I'd chosen to deny, because it was Sam I loved, not Saul.

In short, we saw how our respective families had influenced our ability to relate. After a few sessions, we decided we'd resolved as much as we could have. And beyond this, we agreed, was another challenge: despite our rapturous lovemaking and the fun we had together, we often experienced a tension in our relationship that neither of us knew how to talk about. Nor was the counselor able to help us access the problem.

It was raining outside one evening while Sam and I were eating dinner on the rug by the fire. "Have you done any thinking about the Mother and meditation training?" I asked.

He frowned and smacked his lips. "I think that's your path, Luce, not mine."

My stomach knotted. Following a long silence, Sam broke out with a funny story about one of the prisoners.

Only a few snatches of his tale managed to filter through the haze of my mind. "Sam, aren't you avoiding something?"

He stopped chewing and looked at his plate. "Maybe."

I felt lonely, hurt, at a loss about what to do or say.

Sam rubbed my foot. "Let's do something special for your birthday. It's next week, right?"

Sam took me to La Paloma for a birthday dinner. I'd never had so many rich hors d'oeuvres—fried oysters, ground meat wrapped in fig leaves, stuffed olives, marinated shrimp. After a couple of glasses of wine, Sam shuffled his chair around so that he faced me straight on, then he clasped my hand. "This is where Saul took you. That's why I brought you here. I needed to break the spell he had on you. I want you back, Luce. I want to know you're mine forever."

I was stunned. *He's still feeling pain over my betrayal. No wonder he's been tense!* Tears welled up in my eyes. "I am yours, Sam."

"How can I be sure?"

I stroked his cheek. "You want to know something? I think we're scared, because we love each other more than we've ever loved anyone. It's something neither of us really understands. Each of us is trying to get at the center of the mystery—you through the vision quest, and I with the Mother. So what are we going to do?"

Sam looked down, took another sip of wine. "We haven't done the big vision quest yet."

I bit into my banana cream pie, sucking loudly.

Sam grinned, dipped his fingers into the pie, and dabbed some on his tongue. Then he squeezed off a piece with his fingers and slipped it into my mouth. We giggled, and I held his sticky fingers to my lips.

He bunched the pink linen napkin into a wad, dipped it into the water glass, washed my face with it, then wiped his hands. "Listen to this. I've been mulling it over for a few days. I want to sit with you at your altar. I want you to teach me to meditate in the way the Mother taught you."

At home few nights later, Sam was attempting to fold his legs into meditation position. "I can't sit like this. How do you do it, anyway?"

I tossed him some pillows. "Sit on a few of these. It'll help until you get used to it. Don't worry—the first few times we'll sit for only ten minutes."

"You're going to take me along bit by bit, huh? That's a relief."

He soon began meditating with me a couple of times a week. In the beginning we breathed and sat quietly for short stretches, then longer ones, until by April we were sitting for forty-five minutes at a time. Already deeply connected on many levels, I found that this practice further harmonized our relationship, and Sam agreed. There was an effortlessness to whatever we did—stepping out to a movie, eating at a restaurant, taking a hike, or even going our separate ways to work.

Meditation also enhanced our expressions of physical love. Inspired by feelings that first arose the night of our altercation over Saul, we'd lie in each other's arms, Sam's lips pressed to my forehead. We'd remain still for a long time, fondling each other's bodies with the tips of our fingers as though playing a Beethoven symphony or a Chopin prelude. We drank the nectar of love through touch alone, without engaging in the usual forms of lovemaking. Bubbling brooks widened into streams, then into rivers cascading to the ocean; amid swells rising and falling, a rapture coursed through us, spiraling up to the moon, spinning out to the stars, and splashing into the universe. Even by day we played in the Garden of Eden, partaking of its fruits and waters. The purity of our love spread to everyone we came in contact with, a sprinkle of rosebuds pouring into the hearts of all.

In mid-May, after completing two more weekend trainings, Sam and I left for our big vision quest, including a four-day solo expedition at the North Rim of the Grand Canyon. Temperatures, we knew, would be ranging from 35 degrees at night to 65 or more during the day—warmer than usual for this time of the year. As we drove toward Phoenix beneath an orange sunrise, I could not help but notice that the saguaros lining the freeway were brown at the base, dying from automobile exhaust fumes.

Something else was bothering me as well. Both Sam and I had had recurring mountain lion dreams during our weekend outings. After some discussion, we concluded that the great cat was a symbol of our journey, and not something to worry about, even though the cougar in one of my dreams had blood dripping from its mouth.

"Tell me your last mountain lion dream again," I asked Sam.

His brow furrowed ever so slightly. "Come on, Luce, this vision quest is going to be fine. We just have to be cautious, that's all. Pee around your site; pray to the six directions; do the buddy thing. Ben, Diana, and the ranger I've spoken with will know where to find us if for any reason we don't get back on time. We can't let ourselves be scared off because of some vague omen." Gripping the steering wheel, he peered through the windshield. "Anyway, I'd rather have an encounter with a wild animal than a wild person, like you did in the Chiricahuas."

I giggled. "I know what that one's like. Okay, I'll stop worrying." We drove on and chatted about his prison job and my counseling.

In Flagstaff we turned onto Highway 89 and headed north through a forest of ponderosa pines, down into the desert again, and onto the Navajo Reservation. In silence we sped through Mother Earth's barren flatland dotted with mesas and occasional rock formations. Navajo Bridge marked the end of the long journey through the desert. From the bridge, the great Colorado River wound like a ribbon through the deep gorge that would widen into the Grand Canyon.

Curving up through stretches of ponderosa pines and junipers, then spruces and firs, we could see large patches of snow on north-facing slopes. Quaking aspens, still bare from winter, stood out against the evergreens like puffs of smoke. At Jacob Lake we dipped into the freezing water and out again as fast as we could—completing a sacred bath before paying homage at the Grand Canyon en route to our base camp area.

I had seen pictures of the canyon and knew that the South Rim was in the Sonoran Desert zone, at an altitude of about 7,000 feet, with cactus, piñon pines, junipers, and groves of ponderosa, whereas the North Rim rose to about 8,000 feet at the canyon's edge and 9,000 on the Kaibab Plateau. It was at the lodge by the edge of the canyon that we pulled into a parking lot and set off on foot down a trail through a dense spruce-fir forest. There I was thrust into the naked grandeur of the place, where millions of years of nature's handiwork stood carved into cathedrals of rock. No postcard had prepared me for the majesty of creation I saw before me.

Afterward, we drove eight miles down a bumpy dirt road to the designated spot—a remote site on a southerly slope covered with aspens, white firs, and blue spruce trees. In the waning hours of twilight we pitched our tent under a fir tree just yards from a meadow still brown from winter. While I cooked dried chicken soup and basmati rice on our camp stove, Sam set about collecting wood and building a fire pit, lining the upper part of it with a bed of rocks to radiate heat. Before long, we were sitting on a huge log in front of the campfire, bundled in down jackets and wool hats, eating and gazing at the flames.

Sam poked the embers with a stick and reviewed the plan: "We'll explore the area together for the first couple of days, stay out alone for four nights, then come back and spend the last day resting as we share our experiences. Once we've chosen our sites, we'll show them to each other, then build really good lean-tos latticed with layers of ferns, needles, and leaves for insulation. We'll construct each hut near a clearing, with its entrance facing the rising sun and with a southerly exposure. We'll do the best we can to use the trees for cover and the sun for warmth. While burning wood, we'll be sure to keep the flames low so as not to start a forest fire.

"The weather's usually clear this time of year, but it's going to be cold. We'll have to collect rocks for our fire pits from high places so they'll be dry; otherwise, we should use mud for a heat reflector. Then we'll bring four gallons of water to each place. The water will probably freeze overnight, but we can thaw it out in the sun, or over hot coals. As for food, we'll carry only four oranges apiece, one for each day; the rest of the time, we'll drink lots of water. Once we're out there, we'll stay within about a thirty-foot radius of the sacred circle, and not roam around. The idea is to get a vision, and to avoid diverting our minds from that goal."

On the first night out alone, I sank into a radiant calm, the sort of inner peace nature often inspires. With marks of urine surrounding my site, my bush shelter nestled under two little fir trees, and Sam not too far away, I felt secure. Sitting inside my sacred circle, just feet from the glowing fire pit, I meditated for a couple of hours. Then the sound of coyotes yipping in the distance took me back to my day in the Chiricahuas. With that came an urgent yearning to see the Mother again, an inner burning that brought tears to my eyes.

The next day, I was irritable and had a headache from lack of food. I remembered Sam saying it would help to drink lots of water, so I did. I then laid out in the sun, basking like a lizard to stay warm. That night, my craving to see the Mother became so great that tears bubbled up through a crevice deep inside me—a place I'd never known existed. Mingled with a pleasurable yearning to know who the Mother really was came an aching desire for Sam to experience her as I did. Kneeling and placing my palms together, I pleaded with her to reveal herself. Then I sang: "Mother, can you hear me . . . Through tears, I'm calling out your name . . . Let me see you now, clearly in my mind . . . Mother, have mercy . . . answer my prayer."

Half expecting her to appear, I squinted at the moon, then scanned the silvery tops of firs. "Please, Mother, I don't understand this sort of longing. You've already told me a great deal about you, but please tell me more." I held my breath, waiting, but she was nowhere to be seen. Something about her elusive comings and goings, her inconsistent appearances when I'd place my palms together, and her message that she was always with me led me to wonder if she was perhaps somewhere inside me. So I closed my eyes and began to search the forest of my mind—a dense and foggy place that had no end. My inner quest was interrupted by a distant, low-pitched growling, almost like a cough, raising goose bumps on the back of my neck. *What animal can that be?*

By day three, I was feeling light-headed and free of irritability. My mind had quieted considerably—so much so that in the early morning a handful of deer came within five feet of me to graze in the clearing. Not once did they take notice of me as I sat very still, leaning against a blue spruce just outside my sacred circle.

That night I returned to the blue spruce and cried again to be with the Mother, a deep sobbing that produced the same inexplicable rapture I'd felt the night before. Once more I prayed, "Please show me who you really are," then sang, "Let me see you now, clearly in my mind . . . Mother, have mercy . . . answer my prayer."

A coyote's high-pitched wail was cut off abruptly by a rattling scream of a sort I'd never before heard, which sent icy tingles up my back. *Is this the same animal I heard last night?* Crouching, I searched through the shadows cast by the filmy light of the full moon. A clamoring hum came suddenly from above, and although I looked up to catch sight of its source, I saw nothing but billions of stars and the disc of the moon.

Now the howling returned, accompanied by a squeal. *A big animal killing a small one?* Then—*zzzzz*—something huge, bright, and sizzling zoomed across the sky and hovered above me. *A meteor? But meteors don't hover in place.* I fell flat to the ground, trying to pretend I wasn't there, and crawled toward my sacred circle. *Why didn't I just stay here in the first place, instead of meditating under the tree?* The hair on my arms stood on end; my lips and tongue felt parched and swollen.

The sizzling object now began to emit a light brighter than the moon overhead. *God, could it be a spaceship?* Inch by inch, I continued to pull myself toward the circle like a snake winding through ferns and across spruce needles. There the buzzing, now resembling the sound I'd heard in my ears while in Hawaii, was less frightening—almost pleasant in fact—and I felt bold enough to sneak a second look. To my amazement, it was no spacecraft that greeted my eyes, but rather a womanlike figure with long black hair and many arms and hands, floating in the air above me and looking very much like the image in the dream I'd had months before. I shaded my eyes from the brilliant light that surrounded her. She wore a red silken garment lined with gold, and in her hands were several objects—a sword, a trident, a mace, and a discus—none of which had been clear in the dream. The most astonishing thing was that her tongue hung out, long, red, and terrifying.

She spoke: "You have asked to know who I am."

My voice trembled and my body shook with fear. "Mother, can it be you?"

With that she grew to an impossible size and shone with an even more blinding light, cast by a million suns radiating all at once from universes inside of her. Rapidly, she flashed forth images of evolutionary creation from cells to fish, frogs to lizards, cave humans to present civilization. She then parted her lips and thousands of human beings, beasts, and birds flew into her mouth like moths into a flame, some catching in the gaps between her teeth. Among them were people I knew: Ben, Diana, Saul, my professors, even Sam. My stomach twisted and turned as my entire past, including every one of my negative feelings and actions—quarrels with my mom, disagreements with friends, violent thoughts, and brutal skirmishes—rose from a chamber deep inside me, swirling up to my esophagus and finally pouring out through my mouth in a fountain of watery mucus. I collapsed on the ground, covered in sweat, swimming in my own liquid. "Mother," I cried out, "please take pity on me. Explain this horrible vision."

She gyrated, waving and clashing her weapons with her many arms, then landed feet-first on the ground, shaking the earth with her dance, her enormous ankle bells jangling with an ear-shattering ring. She roared: "I am the Mother of time, devouring the entire universe! In the beginning I create all worlds, then I preserve them, and in the end I devour them, before creating anew."

I struggled to my knees, quivering and shaking, the land beneath me rippling with each step she took. Holding my palms together, I forced out the words: "Mother, thank you for showing me this vision, but please stop now and return to the form I know. I was foolish to have asked for such a thing. Please, Mother, take away this terrible sight!"

Within seconds the Mother had come back to her human size, and was seated beside me, wearing her usual white cloth and smiling. I sucked in air and scooted away. She giggled as she always did, her teeth shining in the moonlight. I stared in disbelief as she urged me to come closer. When I had inched to within her reach, she drew me to her and, with her hand on my head, coaxed me to rest in her lap. I stiffened and tried to pull away, but she held me fast, stroking my back, mumbling the now familiar, "Shi, shi, shi," until my heartbeat returned to normal. At last I sighed, and relaxed into her embrace. She wiped the sweat from my brow with the cloth that was draped around her head, and covered me with my sleeping bag. Then I dozed off as she sang in a soft whisper, her fingers stroking my hair and face while a breeze rippled through the firs.

Chapter Nine

Offer Me
a Flower

Sam was stroking my back lightly when I awoke. For minutes my mind remained immersed in the night's experience, images of the Mother's terrifying form reeling through my brain. I rolled over and opened my mouth to speak, but Sam put his finger to his lips and whispered, "I couldn't wait for your buddy signal. That was a pretty big earthquake we had last night. I just wanted to make sure you were okay."

Earthquake? I nodded, stunned that we'd had the same experience, although apparently he had no idea *why* the earth shook so violently. He kissed me on the forehead, rose to his feet, and disappeared into the spruce grove.

As I settled back down, I noticed a peculiar sensation of being absent from myself, similar to the "witnessing" I'd perceived in Hawaii. The part of me that felt and thought no longer seemed to occupy my body. Instead, feelings and thoughts simply meandered through me like visitors. I was a heartbeat, a primordial form of life in which everything was visible, as if through translucent flesh. My empty mind expanded, enjoying the warmth of the rising sun in an entirely new way. Boundaries had dissolved, and the blood of the universe was pulsing through all things in equal measure. I was in everything and everything was in me, providing assurance that no harm could come to me.

Something must have lifted me to my feet, because suddenly there I was standing, my body light and airy. Walking took place on its own; breathing seemed to happen through my pores. Every inch of my body was alive, sparkling, like helium. I don't know what kept me from floating away—perhaps bones and flesh, or some covenant to stay.

Smiling, I spun around in the grass and slowly, gently fell onto my back. A hummingbird whirred inches above me, and I raised my finger toward it. The bird accepted the invitation, perched there briefly, flashing its iridescent green breast, then darted away to continue its search for nectar. *Ah, all of life is a search for nectar.* A particular kind of "I"— or eye—pervaded everything, serving simultaneously as experiencer and object experienced, regarding each life form in my midst with a pleasant dispassion.

I reflected on the terrible vision of the Mother. Was she indeed the cause of all things, including my obsession with Saul and Sibyl, my terror in the cave, and beyond that, death and destruction? Clearly, I'd had to plunge into the nether regions in order to feel this dispassionate love for everything around me. Perhaps the constant whirling of ecstasy and despair had been alternately pulling me away from this steady calmness at my core—and ultimately, back to it.

Drawn to the edge of the circle, I stopped abruptly, for there on the ground was an enormous paw print just outside the pee line, and yards beyond it three or four more. I knelt down to examine the marks. They were roundish, with the large dots characteristic of cats, which led me to believe these were cougar prints. Although my mind registered the potential for danger, I felt no fear—only interest.

I spent the rest of the day propped against the spruce tree, marveling at nature's creation. A gray squirrel darted across my legs, tickling me. Pine siskins, their breasts streaked with tan, hopped and chirped inches away. In the distance flickers pecked on tree trunks. After dark, I lay awake for hours studying the stars and the shadows on trees. An owl hooted, then silently swooped after its prey. When I closed my eyes, I was surprised to find a calming and brilliant light flooding my inner vision, an ocean of sun more intense than in Hawaii.

On the last day of our quest, after only a few hours of sleep, I was awakened by a chorus of birds announcing the first light. Nothing felt changed from the day before. I continued to sense a subtle union between viewer and viewed, myself and the world. Every move I made was natural and easy. But as I rolled my sleeping bag and gathered empty water bottles and camping supplies into my pack, I felt a sudden restlessness. Memories of the low-pitched growling and the rattling scream that had accompanied my vision of the red Mother filtered into my mind. A Clark's nutcracker scolded nearby. *I hope Sam's all right.* In spite of feeling ill at ease, I proceeded with my farewell ritual, returning the stones of my sacred circle to random settings under bushes and trees. Then I sat under the spruce to sing: "You are creation . . . You are Creator . . . You are the breath of life in all nature." With a twinge of sadness at leaving my vision-quest paradise, I meandered down the hill, all the while bothered by a nagging in my chest.

Sam and I were to meet at our base camp around seven o'clock. I arrived early, slipped the gear off my back, and set about boiling water for rice porridge to break our fast. By seven-thirty, Sam still had not appeared. *Where is he?* We had agreed not to check the buddy signpost on the last day, since we would be seeing each other at breakfast. But now my stomach turned. With my sense of calm rapidly fading, I threw into the day pack a couple of oranges, a thermos of tea, and fresh water, then I checked the first-aid supplies.

My eyes kept searching the trees Sam was likely to emerge from. Soon I started pacing like an animal. *Maybe he's fallen and broken his leg, or knocked himself out. Maybe a snake bit him.* As I dug through my pack to make sure the snake-bite kit was there, as well as my bandanna to use as a tourniquet, a raven brushed through the air just inches from my head. *Something's definitely wrong.* I stumbled to my feet. The raven cawed. Half falling, half running, I hurried up the hill toward Sam's site. As I approached, something in the air felt ominous—a silence too still for comfort.

I burst through the spruce grove and gasped. "Sam!" He lay sprawled inside his sacred circle, his face smeared with blood, his down jacket ripped and bloody. On the left side of his chest was a gaping wound the size of two fists put together. His left arm was mangled, with bone showing through the torn flesh. *It must have been the lion!*

I rested my ear against his chest. *Please let him be alive!* Although he was warm, I couldn't detect a heartbeat. *Oh, Mother. Please.* Trembling, I reached for the side of his neck, tried to clear my head, to concentrate. Touching his vein, I found him barely pulsing with life. *Thank God.*

My head swam as I tried to focus. *I must stop him from losing more blood!* Instinctively, I applied pressure both to the inner side of his left arm and under his collarbone until the bleeding from his arm and chest slowed. All the while, I prayed: "Mother, please help us." I grabbed the pack and pulled out my bandanna. With my pocketknife, I cut away the sleeve of Sam's jacket and shirt, then the long underwear beneath it, and wrapped the bandanna around his upper arm. I tied a stick inside the knot, as I'd learned to do in our first-aid sessions, twisted it slightly, then secured it with another knot. *I mustn't forget about shock! I've got to keep him warm.* I raced to Sam's lean-to, dragged his sleeping bag out, and spread it over his legs, as well as the right side of his chest.

My every move seemed to take an eternity, especially now that Sam was again losing blood from his chest. The oozing, however, indicated a shallow wound. *Thank God for your down jacket and long johns—otherwise that lion might have taken a deeper bite.* I cut away the clothing from his chest, nearly fainting from the sight of so much torn flesh. *I've got to concentrate.* After taking deep breaths to steady myself, I tore a piece from the cut-off fabric of his shirt, placed it on the chest wound, and applied direct pressure under his collarbone until the bleeding slowed once more. *Antiseptic! I've got to clean the wound.* I fished around my pack for the iodine, and began to dab it around the edges of the chest wound, careful not to aggravate the bleeding. At this point Sam began to moan. I rubbed his face with mine, mingling tears with his blood. "I know it hurts, Sam. I'm here. Everything's going to be all right."

I had no idea how to dress the enormous chest wound. Then all at once I remembered scenes from a movie in which pieces of cloth were tied together, with other pieces underneath, to make a compress. I laid gauze over the wound and scraps of jacket over that, then cut apart another of Sam's shirts to make a bandage, sliding the strips of cloth under him, and wrapping it snugly around. I felt hopeful with the wound now covered, but as a precaution I again applied pressure under his collarbone.

Now the arm splint. Breaking a stick the size of a broom handle, I set about padding it with fragments of Sam's parka, then lightly tied the whole thing into place. I stroked his head and examined the scratches on his cheek. They were deep yet thin, made no doubt by claws, rather than teeth. Largely clotted over, they were bleeding only slightly. After cleaning them, I used butterflies made of adhesive tape to patch the skin together as best I could.

After positioning Sam's sleeping pad an inch or so from his head, I locked my elbows under his armpits and, inch by careful inch, dragged him onto it. At least now he wouldn't be losing precious body heat to the cold ground. He groaned and grimaced. Running my fingers through his hair, I said, "I know this is hard, Sam. We have to keep you warm." With that done, I stuffed his empty back-pack under the pad to raise his head and chest, and again spread his sleeping bag over him.

Huddled beside him, I rubbed his good arm, stared at his face, and wondered if the lion would return to finish its kill. Then I lifted my head to search for signs of a tussle, noting only a few stones out of place on the perimeter of the sacred circle, along with some drag marks, but no lion prints—at least not close by.

Loosening the tourniquet, I kissed Sam on the check and stroked his forehead. "Sam, can you hear me?"

He groaned and tried to lift his right arm.

I held onto him and rocked gently. "That's okay. Just let me know you're all right."

His lips parted slightly, then he moaned and went limp.

Quickly, I checked his wrist; his pulse was barely detectable. *How am I going to get him out of here? Mother, now is the time to come. Please help us.* Not knowing what else to do I checked his wrist every so often. I thought up new words to a song on my favorite tape and sang, "Oh, holy Mother, comfort me. Let me hear you once more whisper my name. Please come again and lead us to safety." Over and over again, I sang it, like a lullaby to soothe Sam's pain.

Remembering the importance of massaging an injured person to stimulate their circulation and bring them out of shock, I began to rub his legs, feet, and good arm. His fingers weakly clasped my hand as I kneaded his palm. "Sam? I love you."

I wondered how this terrible accident could possibly bring us closer to the immortal nectar. Did Sam have to die for me to fully understand the immortality of the soul? My vision of him, along with everyone else I knew, racing into the devouring Mother's mouth let me know this calamity could signify the end of him, and of us. *Oh, Mother, I can't live without him.* Holding my head, I rocked back and forth, trying to enter the calm I now knew lay beneath my despair.

At about noon, when the sun was in the midheaven, Sam's pulse gained strength. I took the opportunity to collect food, cooking utensils, my sleeping bag, and some tarps, from our base camp. Once back at Sam's site, I rigged the big tarp from the trees above him, all the while softly repeating, "Sam, please be okay." Since the surrounding trees were too far apart to support a lean-to, I set about building a semicircular wall behind him for shelter. By pounding two rows of large sticks into the ground, I created a space between the branches, which I then filled in with a latticework of needles, leaves, and ferns.

Occupied with weaving sticks and debris, my mind stayed focused on the task before me; even so, it was impossible to hold back the ache that rose in waves from my chest. Then I gave my mind and body another task: digging a fire pit by Sam's feet. As I worked, rumbles and flashes along the horizon signaled rain. Soon clouds were gathering and the breeze was picking up speed, causing the tarp to flap about wildly.

By late afternoon, Sam had started to mumble incoherently. After checking his pulse, which seemed far more steady, I decided the danger of shock had passed and he was in need of water and sustenance. Removing the water bottle from my pack, I lifted his head. "Here's a little water," I coaxed, touching the spout to his lips. I dripped some into his mouth, and he swallowed slowly. Then I cut an orange slice and held it to his lips. "Can you can suck on this?" He took in a little, then his lips moved, but I couldn't make out his words. Once again I nestled close to keep him warm, every once in a while checking his pulse.

Just before dusk, I tightened the tarp and got the fire going in the pit. On our miniature camp stove I heated water for chicken broth and held a cup of it to Sam's lips. "Can you drink some of this soup?" I asked. He mumbled and sipped a little. I then soaked a piece of bread in the broth and slipped it into his mouth. He half-opened his eyes and again tried to speak, but continued to utter sounds that made no sense to me. I stroked his body once more. "Don't worry," I reassured him. "You're going to be okay." Soon he drifted off to sleep. As darkness fell, the fire reflecting off the bush wall warmed us.

Half dreaming, half awake, I saw, as clearly as if in Technicolor, my childhood encounter with the wolf and with the Mother. She *did* deliver my wish for a paradise with a swan princess, a land of joy and delight, as we made angels in the snow. Then she came again in the Chiricahuas. *My God, what love! I had no idea my desire for it would bring such suffering.* Surely, I thought, this couldn't be the end, for now Sam was my prince and I was about to enter the magical kingdom as his princess. Was that the Mother's lesson—that I myself am the swan princess? *If so, Mother, then please keep him alive.*

After examining Sam's bandages by flashlight and finding no signs of fresh blood, I added my sleeping bag to the covers and cuddled up beside him. Keeping watch as I lay there, I heard pieces of the wall's insulation blowing off in the wind and Sam groaning in his sleep. Every now and then I stroked his forehead and his hair, wondering what to do if the lion returned. Then I remembered that wild animals steer clear of fires, so I got up to build ours higher, rising again every so often to feed it. All the while, I tried to imagine Sam's encounter with the cougar. Why had it chosen him instead of me? Why had it grabbed his chest rather than his throat? Maybe it didn't intend to kill him— at least not right away. I peered into the forest, listening for sounds, imagining a pair of cat eyes out there glowing in the dark.

Sometime past midnight Sam began to moan loudly, tossing his head, and flailing his good arm. He was flaming hot with fever. I hurried over to our supplies, dipped a cloth in water, and began to mop his forehead with it. "You're going to be okay, Sam. Someone will come." I was convinced help would be on its way, since the ranger would suspect trouble if we failed to check out of the Grand Canyon the next morning as expected, and since Ben and Diana knew our return date and would alert the forest service if we didn't show up. *But that might be too late.* Once again I held Sam's wrist to check his pulse. The fever must have weakened him, because his pulse was thin and seemed to skip beats. The wind now screamed through the spruces and firs, shaking the latticework, blowing off bits of debris, and rippling the tarp till I thought everything would break loose. A few cold droplets flew under the tarp and hit my face. *How will I keep him warm and dry in this storm?* Coyotes howled in the distance. A chill coursed through my veins as I gazed into the starless night.

I must have drifted off to sleep, for the next thing I knew, it was morning. The fire had gone out and a corner of the tarp had ripped free. The wind had calmed a bit, leaving the sky dark gray and the air hazy with mist. When I sat up to check Sam's wounds, I was startled to see a figure approaching in the distance. The back of my neck tingled. Nevertheless, hoping it might be a hiker who could help, I leapt up and raced forward. But within seconds I could tell this was like no hiker I'd ever seen. Large, broad shouldered, and clothed in a black robe with a monklike cowl, the stranger marched as though to the slow cadence of a drum. I stopped, waved my arms, and shouted, but the black-robed figure merely trudged forward, dirgelike, never changing its pace. As it drew closer, the hair on my arms stood on end. Suddenly feeling like a trapped animal, I bolted back to the bush wall. Arriving out of breath, I stood in front of Sam and faced the dark being that approached with the unrelenting momentum of death itself.

The hooded form, which appeared to be a man, mounted the small rise just below the site, stepping firmly over the rocks marking the border of the sacred circle. With my muscles suddenly drained of their strength, I involuntarily backed away. The figure halted at Sam's feet. Towering over him like a vulture, the hooded stranger raised his arms toward the sky, mumbling a rhythmic chant. Beads of sweat stung my eyes as I sank to my knees and vomited.

When I looked up again, the man had pulled a hairy rope out of the cloth purse slung across his chest. He then tied it into a noose and bent over Sam, at which point I surged upright and dove between them, spreading my arms like wings. "No!" I shouted.

The robed figure stepped past me and proceeded to lug Sam by the feet into the open. There he slipped the noose around Sam's chest, then hoisted the rope over his shoulder, and bending like a reaper, began to drag Sam away.

"He's hurt. You can't do that!" I yelled, but the man paid no attention. In a panic, I picked up a stick, intending to strike him, but my upraised arm became paralyzed in midair, as though by some invisible grip. The cloaked figure resumed his slow march. Letting the stick fall from my hand, I ran in front of them, where I toppled to the ground, blown like a leaf by the wave of his hand.

Pulling myself up, I stumbled behind, weeping, "No, you can't have him!" Catching hold of a tree trunk, I had rested my head on my arms, panting and whimpering, when the howling of distant coyotes renewed my strength. Still reeling, I began to trail after Sam and the reaper.

I pitched forward, following at a distance, never losing sight of them. After a while the black-robed man stopped and turned to look over his left shoulder. He called out in a deep, hollow voice, "Luce, you must not follow."

Although I was startled that he knew my name, his words, full of thunder, filled me with courage and determination. *Who is he? Am I dreaming?* I breathed deeply and surrendered to the fact that whether I was immersed in a highly realistic dream or in real life, I had no choice in this matter: wherever Sam went, I, too, would go.

With my mind set only on survival, I moved along directly behind them. An energy that held fast against my chest, however, kept me from edging up too close. I pushed forward, as if against a stiff wind. Every once in a while, I wrapped my arms around a tree trunk and leaned against it, resting my cheek on the bark. Then I trudged forward again, making my way against the invisible force.

All at once the wind began to blow anew, wailing through the firs and spruces, rippling the figure's robes. I turned and twisted into the gale, driving myself forward. The figure paused beneath a giant spruce, where drooping limbs waved like enormous fans above his hooded head. The top of the tree swayed to and fro against a sky now filled with black clouds. His voice echoed off distant mountains: "I have warned you. You must not follow."

With a strength that was not mine, I stepped in front of him; looked into his terrifying countenance; searched his eyes, two black holes echoing with the screams of millions dying; and asked, "Who are you?"

He boomed: "I am the Lord of Death. I must take your betrothed to another land. It is not destined for you to go there at this time. You must turn back." With that he pulled on the rope, dragging Sam across pine needles and rock.

My body reverberated, pierced by his words. As if bound from head to toe by invisible chains, I struggled to move but could not budge. *Death!* I wondered if I was dead, too—if my wish to be with Sam had carried me beyond the land of the living. Closing my eyes, I grasped at faded images of the Mother and felt her fingers on my back, stroking gently. I reeled in memories of the coyotes in the Chiricahua cave, the Mother sitting under the ponderosa. Now the wind slowed, caressing my face. My now relaxed muscles allowed me to plod forward once again, first one foot, then the other. As I moved, my body softened, and I began stepping lightly through the trees and across the grass, at last freed of the resistant force.

Once again the Lord of Death came to a halt, then swiveled to face me. From under the cowl, his gaze burned into me. He rumbled: "You are a brave and loyal woman. I will give you whatever you wish, but I cannot return Sam to you."

That must mean Sam's dead and I'm not and this is no dream. Propelled by a will that was not my own, I knelt and placed my palms together. My diction sounded archaic to my ears: "O Lord of Death, grant me the wisdom to understand why you must take him away. What has he done? I cannot live unless he also lives. I am nothing without him."

Imperturbable as a statue, the hooded figure bellowed: "Whatever seeds a person plants by his words and his actions, the results must be borne by him. I am only performing the task designed for me by the creatrix. With your divine eye opened, you saw a vision of the Mother of the universe creating, preserving, and then devouring what she had created. Death is inevitable. Therefore, stop following and allow the ordained to take place." His words stamped themselves into my brain as though onto tablets of hidden knowledge.

Then the Lord of Death raised his hand in blessing and turned again, hauling Sam away, scraping his body along the earth like a sweeper. The pounding of timpani filled the air—*boom, boom, boom*—in tempo with my own heartbeat.

I kept to my course, marching a short distance behind the two, fixing my eyes on Death as he dragged Sam's body through gullies and up hills. Void now of thoughts and feelings, I was left with only the urge to pursue.

Once again the Lord of Death came to a standstill, this time in front of a granite boulder. With arms spread out, his sleeves billowing in the wind, he thundered: "I see that you are not afraid. I am obligated to reward you for your courage and wisdom in the face of death. Ask me for anything except the return of your beloved."

My heart swelled with love. Tears of gratitude for I-knew-not-what streamed down my face. I fell to my knees, placed my palms together in prayer, and asked for the one thing that mattered above all else: "O Lord of Death, if you can, please grant me knowledge of the immortal nectar."

Black storm clouds began to swirl in the sky above the mountains. Screaming winds howled through the firs and spruces. Lightning flashed and thunder roared. Rain spilled in sheets, blinding my eyes to Sam and Death. I surged forward, plowing through curtains of rain, shouting, "Ma, Ma, Ma!" Groping through the gray deluge, I staggered this way and that. Then I collapsed, falling into a vision of Sam and me in a green meadow, with flowers raining from the sky and milk cows offering their udders.

When I became aware of my surroundings again, the rumbling thunder had faded into the distance and the sun was warming my face. I opened my eyes, wonder struck. The Mother, in her familiar white robes, held Sam on her lap. A mountain lion lay with eyes half-closed on the ground beside them. A coyote rested next to boulder at the edge of the fir-spruce grove, and a few deer grazed in a nearby meadow, which seemed to turn from brown to green before my eyes. The Mother was kissing Sam's wounds and stroking his face. Caught in a ripple of joy, I struggled to my knees and crawled slowly toward them. Pausing to wipe my tears, I sat on my heels, staring in disbelief. She giggled, beckoned me forward, and held the two of us in her arms for a long time.

While sound asleep with Sam, I was awakened by a loud clattering. A helicopter circled above us, its propeller clacking through the air. I stared at it in amazement, unsure if we were in heaven or on earth. As I surveyed the landscape, everything looked radiant—the blue sky, the afternoon sun, the blue spruces, the gray-white aspens, the bracken ferns. Even the iron bird, topped by its whirling halo, seemed beautiful as it settled into a clearing a mile or so away.

I kissed Sam on the forehead. He opened his eyes partway and, with what seemed like a half smile, grunted in acknowledgment. I sat up, listening for signs of our rescue party. Pulling out waterproof matches from the inside pocket of my jacket, I announced, "I'm going to make a fire so they'll find us." I knelt before a stack of pine needles and dead sticks off trees, lighting several matches before I succeeded in setting the pile ablaze.

As I fanned the flames with my wool hat, I felt as though I were playing a game. After all we'd been through, was it still necessary to worry about whether someone would find us? In my present state of consciousness, the difference between alive and dead did not seem to matter, and certainly did not affect my sense of well-being. Coming face-to-face with Death and Sam's dying had me bowing down to the gift of life and death—and all that issued forth from the Mother's grace. As far as I could tell, nothing could ever go wrong.

Sam's periodic moaning let me know he was still in pain. After tucking my jacket around him to keep him warm, I waited for our rescuers, all the while reflecting on my encounter with the black-robed figure. What enabled me to follow him as he dragged Sam away was the unconditional love and the witnessing form of observation that had taken over, suffusing me with a sense of detachment. Suddenly, I was acting from something inside me that felt greater than myself. This, I knew at last, was the immortal nectar. It was the love and dispassion of the Mother moving in and through me, providing a very natural and normal sense of surrender to my divine self—a feeling of nonseparation from all of creation.

My reflections ended abruptly, for out of the forest came the pilot, two medical technicians, and the forest ranger Sam had phoned before we left Tucson. The tall, lanky ranger greeted me with a broad grin. "When I noticed you were late reporting in, I called the rescue team. Sure glad you're both alive."

My perception of the world around me as one pulsing beat of life had settled into my consciousness permanently—through the helicopter ride home, nights in the hospital with Sam, sessions with clients, and catching up on bills and other household responsibilities. I was aglow with an inner calm untainted by worries or by thoughts of the past or future. Even so, I had to adjust to the new way my mind was operating: thoughts, emotions, and actions were coming through effortlessly, then passing on without leaving a trace. As for my will forces, they arose only when I dabbled in perceptions of separation. Actually, while in the state of oneness, I no longer experienced the old paradox that had differentiated will from fate—everything, including me, was participating effortlessly in the same dance.

I simply smiled when the hospital doctors said they couldn't understand why there was no need to amputate Sam's arm, or why there was no apparent nerve damage, or why Sam had no nightmares, sudden outbursts of fear, or other indications of post-traumatic stress. A blood transfusion was needed, however, as was morphine; and his arm and chest wounds had to be tended to regularly.

After resting for a night and a day, Sam was able to tell me about his experience. I sat on a chair beside his bed. He was quite a sight with the claw marks on his cheeks and forehead, his chest wrapped in bandages, and his arm in a sling dangling from a metal rod. He was suffering, but because he wanted to be aware of every moment possible, he had refused additional painkillers.

He spoke in a weak voice. "I'm not sure how I knew it was a she-lion, but it was. I'd seen her tracks and decided to stay up that last night waiting for my vision. Like I'd told you, I knew I would have one, but I sure had no idea it would be in the flesh." He managed a grin and then continued. "All night I listened intently—to the silence, the occasional growls, her paws breaking a twig now and then. By morning, when I hadn't received a vision, I figured *she* had to be it. Breaking our rule, I went outside the pee circle to follow her tracks, hoping to catch a glimpse of her. It was early, just before sunrise. I was stalking, creeping around in search of her prints, fur on branches, disturbances among the dead leaves and needles. I got so I could *feel* her, and every once in a while I'd catch sight of something tan moving behind a spruce tree, but then I'd think it was only my imagination.

"At one point I believe she really wanted me to see her, because she made rustling sounds in the ferns. Then all at once I spotted her less than ten feet away—yellow eyes staring at me through the gray-white trunks of aspens. God, she was beautiful! After that, I lost all sense of her until thought I heard claws scraping against the bark of a tree behind me. Next thing I knew, she'd jumped me. I wrestled with her like I would with a man. I've never felt so powerful. Even so, I was no match for her. I'll never forget her growl, throaty and deep. There was a strange sense of love when she tore into me—like a communion initiating me into some spirit world. Her kingdom, maybe.

"Anyway, my lion must have thought I was about dead, because she dragged me by the arm and deposited me under a bush right next to the stones marking my sacred circle. Then she went away, probably to bring her cubs. I somehow found the strength to crawl into the circle. That's when you came." Sam touched me lightly with his good hand, his eyes brimmed over with tears.

I rested my hand on his. He continued: "I guess I was delirious, though I do remember thinking the lion must have been leading me around a big loop the whole time I was stalking her. That night as I lay beside you, I was fading in and out, dreaming of her, thrilled that I'd found my power animal at last. I think I went unconscious a few times before feeling your head on my chest or your fingers massaging me. Then there was a long tunnel, like those that dying people often describe, and at the end of it a brilliant light. At first, I was overcome with joy; then instantly, everything went dark and a hooded man appeared, tied a rope around my chest, and began dragging me off. I seemed to be above my body yet in it, too. Then I heard you yelling, 'No, you can't have him.' The more he dragged me, the more my corpse felt like a sack of bones and flesh—not at all important. And

I began to think this man in robes was my best friend, like an angel
or something, and was taking me on a journey to show me that only
joy is real." At that point Sam began to weep like a baby.

I held him for a long time, and when he stopped crying, his eyes
were bright as diamonds. "Soon a storm came," he went on. "I knew
my body was getting wet, but I couldn't feel a thing. Then I heard you
calling, 'Ma, Ma, Ma.' Next thing I knew, the sun was out and I was
in my body again. Then the weirdest thing happened: I smelled roses!
The ground was soft like a feather bed, and someone was dabbing my
wounds with rosebuds. Was that you? Where did you find roses?"

I leaned over and kissed the scratches on his cheek. "The
Mother was holding you and touching her lips to your wounds. She
often smells like roses."

He was still for a minute, then turned his head to look at me.
"Is that for real?"

I combed my fingers through his hair and whispered: "I had passed
out and had a dream about us. When I came to, I saw the Mother
holding you. Your she-lion and my coyote were also there. Then the
Mother drew the two of us onto her lap. Didn't you see her, Sam?"

He scratched his head and closed his eyes for a minute. "No,
just the smells and touch, and the extraordinary feeling of love, like
God or something."

When Sam was discharged from the hospital, he came to stay with
me, and never left. I was deeply moved that he'd felt the Mother's
love. Convinced that vision questing was his way of contacting the
divine, I realized that what he called it didn't matter—the love was
the same, full and complete. He was my swan prince, forever and
beyond. And the Mother was my guide in eternal love.

One morning in early June, while walking just off Pima
Canyon Trail, I stopped to rest beneath a mesquite tree. Everything
before me sparkled with energy, as if outlined by starlight, and I
luxuriated in this view of the world as a place free of separation and
infused with love. Then I began to wonder about subtle drifts of

jealously I'd been feeling, currents of greed and lust, even behaviors that seemed inharmonious with my state of mind.

All of a sudden, the Mother was standing next to me with her hand on my shoulder, repeating the now familiar words, "Shi, shi, shi." Fluidly, she settled cross-legged onto the ground, giggling, then taking me into her arms. The sparkling light in her eyes immediately turned to a deep, dense black. She said: "Child, you must continue your practices until you are fully identified with me. Your eye of knowledge has been opened; you now know that the love flowing through you, through all creation, is the immortal nectar, and is no different from me. But this has not yet become your permanent state.

"For the remainder of your journey, both with Sam and on your own, you must be more vigilant than ever. The traces of negativity you experience from time to time are a part of creation. However, they can still be dangerous. Just as steam is more powerful than water, words and actions arising from negative thoughts and feelings can cause you once more to fall into perceptions of separation. You must therefore strive for compassion.

"Daughter, the purification of your mind and body will continue as you make the effort to be kind, patient, and forgiving. In the absence of pride and anger, you will learn to live with pure, unbounded love. In truth, child, the more humble you become, like a little worm with its belly on the ground, the more the immortal nectar will bubble in your heart. Eventually, it will flow there eternally and you will attain liberation from all sorrow."

A fountain of love poured out of my heart. All I could do was nod and smile.

She stroked my face. "Now you know I am always inside you as well as all around you. As a daily reminder, continue to place your hands in prayer position and then offer me a flower, a leaf—anything bestowed in devotion. These gifts will help you feel my presence."

As she rose and floated down the hill, tears of gratitude washed over my cheeks. She turned and called out, "Child, you must tell your story to those who want to hear it." Her voice echoed in my mind as I watched her disappear behind the giant saguaro cactuses, her white garments flapping in the breeze, fading into the desert like a shimmering mirage.

ABOUT THE AUTHOR

For there to be life, there must be breath; for Savitri, the Mother is that breath. For this reason, she dedicates her life to the path of the Mother.

Savitri L. Bess, transpersonal therapist, workshop facilitator, fiber artist, and devotee of Mata Amritanandamayi, has been following the path of the Mother for twenty-eight years. She first met a motherly spiritual guide at a Pennsylvania retreat in 1971. Eventually, she stayed at this ashram for six months on a National Endowment for the Arts grant to study Tantric art, ultimately renouncing her career as a college instructor to live as a monastic. Over the next nine years, she resided at the ashram, where she taught the philosophy and religion of Hinduism, yoga, and meditation.

In 1980, Savitri, at the behest of her spiritual guide, founded and directed The Center for Creative Consciousness in Tucson, Arizona. Simultaneously, she earned a master's degree in counseling and then opened a private practice that integrated spirituality with conventional therapy techniques. She also obtained a certificate in Holotropic Breathwork and participated in 12-Step programs for adult children of alcoholics.

After closing the yoga center in 1989, Savitri set out to explore her shadow. While living for seven months in a forest hermitage, she gave expression to the "dark feminine" through fiber art. Her shadow journey sparked an art exhibition entitled "Honoring the Dark," as well as a workshop series, "Women's Sacred Art Circle."

In 1992, Savitri met Mata Amritanandamayi (Ammachi), a holy woman believed by many to be the Black Mother Kali incarnate. Savitri's yearning to know the darkest recesses of her own soul, and ultimately to merge with the light of the Mother of the Universe, led her to India, where she lived with Ammachi intermittently for three years. At Ammachi's suggestion, she began writing *The Path of the Mother: Out of the Shadow into Love* at her home in Taos, New Mexico. Later, she received inspiration to write *Offer Me a Flower: A Spiritual Quest*, which she finished after moving to an Ammachi ashram in Santa Fe.

ORDER FORM

Discounts available on orders of 10 or more books.

SHIPPING & HANDLING
US $3.00 for first book; $1.25 for each additional book
Canada $3.60 for first book, $1.50 for each additional book

Please contact your local bookstore or mail your order, together
with your name, address, and personal check or money order, to:

Bharati Impressions
7658-C Old Santa Fe Trail
Santa Fe, NM 87505
To order by credit card, call Blessingway Books, at 800-716-2953